Mireille opened th... mauve negligée. It ... which looked firm ... years of being fondled and s... ... . Florian tilted back her head, she pulled his down, and they kissed lingeringly. She was a tall woman, blonde and somewhat marked by alcohol, sun and the general wear and tear of life, but still attractive. Mireille was hot. Exceptional. She would do it anywhere, any time. And probably with anyone, thought Florian with a trace of bitterness.

LUST IN PARIS

Antoine S.

Translated from the French by
Celeste Piano

NEXUS

A NEXUS BOOK
published by
the Paperback Division of
W. H. Allen & Co. Plc

A Nexus Book
Published in 1986
by the Paperback Division of
W. H. Allen & Co. Plc
Sekforde House, 175/9 St. John Street,
London, EC1V 4LL
Reprinted 1989

First published in France by Editions Robert Laffont under the title
Florian ou le savoir-jouir

Copyright © Editions Robert Laffont, S.A., Paris 1984

Printed and bound in Great Britain by
Cox & Wyman Ltd, Reading

ISBN 0 352 31654 3

In memory of the master, Henry Miller

'Greatness of character does not consist in having no passions. On the contrary, one must possess them to the highest degree yet hold them in check.'

Nietzsche

1

FLORIAN AND GULLIVER

Florian always slept naked, whatever the season, the circumstances or the bed.

That morning he woke up early, tugged awake by Gulliver, which sprang to attention as it invariably did at the start of a new day. The lively creature's fiery, sensitive head was enjoying itself, rubbing against the linen sheet which scratched and tickled it simultaneously, giving rise to a delicious sensation.

His eyes half open and his desire on edge, Florian allowed himself to wallow in the pleasant sensation of this gentle awakening. Thoughts and ideas gradually began to take shape, then darted off like butterflies. Where was he? Whose bed was this? With whom had he spent the night? He stretched out his right arm, then extended the left: no one else on either side.

The mists of the night cleared and the world resumed its familiar contours. He was surfacing, gradually. He recognised the window, the ceiling – with its long crack rather like an aerial photo of the wall of China – the room and all its familiar contents were there, everything in place. He was in his own home.

He checked out the assortment of scents which assailed his nose as it ventured over the edge of the sheet, and sniffed at the air with a series of little inhalations similar to those of an animal emerging from its burrow. When wine-tasting, only very small mouthfuls are required, after which the tastebuds themselves go into action.

In much the same way, Florian was inhaling small measures of air through his nostrils, respiring and exhaling with a subtlety acquired only by many years of olfactory practice.

The predominant aroma at present – the orchestra's big bass drum, so to speak – was that of coffee, a mixture of Robusta and Arabica apparently. Yes, that was it: Arabusta 60%, medium quality and medium ground, imported from Africa. Over this vacuum packed powder had been poured water insufficiently heated.

The robustly Arabic effluvia had climbed three floors and infiltrated beneath four doors before finally reaching the fifty million olfactory neurons nestling in their velvety mucous. Some of the neurons – specialists at detecting alkaloids – transmitted their infinitely complex signals to the brain, after amplifying them a million times. 'Coffee, yes! Arabica, Robusta, filter-style, made with ordinary tap-water, .02% fluoride content.'

But actually Florian was none too bothered about the coffee. While aware of this effect upon his nasal passages, he turned his attention towards a very much subtler odour, that of the day itself. Nostrils aquiver, he evaluated the quality of the air, the atmosphere of a fine spring day. For it promised to be fine indeed, the atmospheric pressure around 1025 millibars, and dry too, hygrometry between 60 and 70%. Florian opened his eyes wide. The sun was filtering through the wooden shutters.

Gulliver however chafed with impatience, head rearing with displeasure at this bachelor's reveille.

'Relax old fellow,' Florian muttered, stroking the warm rounded tip with his fingers casually. He did not linger thus, reserving such pleasures for later. 'Keep calm! The day's just beginning. You'll have your fun today – more than once – if not several times! Pretty girls await us, women are everywhere!'

Each day he would marvel at the thought that every other person in the world was of the female sex. What a wonderfully gluttonous prospect! Hundreds, thousands of trim little buttocks just asking to be caressed, and myriads of lissom legs waiting for one thing only – to dance and kick to the frenzied jig of as many bucking Gullivers.

'Who will I seduce today?' wondered Florian Nazulis, 33, b. Paris, father: clarinettist, mother: maternal; *address*: 69 Rue des Saints-Pères, Paris 6; *height*: 1.74m; *weight*: 72 kilos; *blood group*: A Rhesus Positive; *hair*: light brown; *eyes*: blue; *nose*: aquiline; *status*: twice divorced, 12 times separated, engaged 20 times; *profession*: wine writer and columnist for *Gourmet Magazine*; social security no: 1.51.03.75.129.0014.2; *birthsign*: Scorpio with Leo rising; *astrological characteristics*: problems with women, chiefly sexual instability, hyper-energetic; *psychological aspects*: prone to neurosis, calls his genital organ Gulliver, apparently converses with and listens to it. Case history gives cause for alarm. Does not look after himself properly.

'Who'll I seduce today?' Nazulis wondered, stretching out his arms in a languorous imitation of a javelin thrower, accompanied by a lengthy yawn that turned into an Indian war-whoop.

Now he was wide awake. Today, Tuesday 24th April 1984, latitude 48°N by longitude 2°E, what new pleasures lay in store? What wines, culinary delicacies, music? And, primarily, what women?

2

THE NEIGHBOUR, SCHUBERT
AND MIREILLE

Out of the darkness, a stunning female body, toffee-coloured and stark naked, appeared in the doorway to the bedroom. Nazulis, his eyes wrinkling in astonishment, recognised her.

'Oh, Lea!' he exclaimed.

A long silken mane of hair cascaded down past the small of her back, as far as the tiny golden-brown buttocks. Black eyes sparkling out of the darkness. Curve of shoulders, diminutive youthful breasts jutting proudly – yes, it was Lea, the Eurasian, with her languorous liana-like suppleness. And that tongue of hers: a nonchalant rasp! A strange smile played upon her moist lips. She drew closer and opened her mouth slightly. Her little pink tongue flickered like a serpent's . . .

Gulliver quivered in an electric surge, hoarding all the ardour of the morning hard-on.

Then suddenly replacing the vision, there followed another, this time strong and strapping, right in front of Florian's astonished nose. Here were the magnificent haunches of the young German girl: the real rump of a natural blonde – pink, with flaxen down. What was her name? Greta, Hilde, Martha? Florian wracked his brains, but he was bad at remembering names. A splendid, imposing athletic bottom that had been, in the Teutonic tradition of the Valkyries, with ample cheeks in whose centre blossomed the hairy bouquet, that fine golden sheaf.

It was the type of rear at which he loved to thrust, bucking and battering vigorously, with Martha or Greta or Birgitta or whatever her name was, lying spreadeagled, face down. She would part her legs somewhat and raise her arse and he, foraging through the blonde thatch, would thrash his way into her, working away with ever-wilder cudgelling blows. 'More, more, more!' she would groan, gasping gutturally and interspersing the command with moans of 'Ach!' or 'Noch!' which might turn into 'Nein!' and finally 'Ja! Ja! Ja!' The latter exclamatory triad formed the three final steps of that orgasmic staircase she was squealingly climbing while she bit the mattress, ground her teeth and dribbled over the sheets.

Deeply embedded inside her, and on his knees, he would regain his breath, gasping like a marathon runner. On filling his lungs once again, he would resume, Gulliver by now quite demented. He gripped her firm, rounded bum, accompanied by trumpets, tubas, horns and Wagnerian trombones in an endless crescendo, a wild Germanic gallop towards the yellow and black clouds of a Valkyrie sunset which finally faded out altogether in his memory.

Then everything became silent and peaceful again. A drop of water rolled along a leaf and fell on to a stone, then another followed suit. Beatrice's dazzling features swam into view, that ambiguous, fascinating green-eyed inquisitive look of hers: ah Beatrice, gentle redhead whose milky skin was sown with freckles! She too promptly disappeared, vanishing somewhere in her land of dreams. (In fact, she had ditched Florian Nazulis for an Italian she had fallen in love with, a rich exporter of pasta.) And now, making her appearance on stage, was the perfect body of that Negress, whose particular aroma was of musk and warm pastry, and who had been exquisitely baked by centuries of solar cuisine. She it was who brought him swiftly to the vertical, with her peppery scent and her woolly-tufted oxters into which he loved to sink his nose and indulge in an olfactory truffling full of savour, thence downward to the coarsely-haired nest, which he opened with the tip of his tongue, thus flushing out the scarlet fledglings . . .

His eyes smarted with these images. Florian

got out of bed and placed his feet on the threshold of a new morning full of a host of possibilities. How good it was to be alive! And how strong desire is!

He uttered a sort of joyful growl and with a single rapid motion flung open the shutters, which banged against the wall, making the whole building vibrate.

His eyes dazzled by the sudden sunlight, and Gulliver still stiffly in evidence, Florian casually waved hello at the silhouetted figure framed in the window opposite. Startled by the noisy clatter of shutters, this silent form was now motionless. Florian gradually distinguished its outline, shading his eyes with a hand like a sea-captain scrutinising the horizon.

It was a woman.

With one hand to her mouth in her astonishment at seeing this muscularly naked man flourishing a spectacular erection.

The sun picked out the prick extended like a veritable hammer so that it cast a huge shadow against the pale yellow background of the bedroom. It resembled some projectile, a missile of sorts, a demonic vision from which she could not avert her gaze.

'Good morning neighbour!' Nazulis cried.

She did not answer.

Her eyes looked extraordinarily round and her attractive features were fringed by chestnut curls which fell on to the collar of her blue quilted dressing gown. She was indeed delightful.

'Hello, good morning, dear neighbour whose name I don't know,' intoned Florian.

'Good morning, Monsieur,' she replied in a clear but not loud voice.

Blushing and embarrassed, she turned her back as if to retreat.

'Wait!' Nazulis shouted. 'Don't go! You're my nymph of the morning, the radiant visage of the dawn . . . The charm of . . . of . . . well, to be honest, I like you.'

She was looking at him hesitantly.

'Come and have a cup of coffee,' he suggested, pulling on his dressing gown. (Curtains for Gulliver, for the time being.) 'What a lovely day! Ah, spring!' This with an expansive gesture towards the sky.

She made as if to shut the window.

'Wait, wait! Coffee, tea, chocolate, alcohol, hashish, sweeties . . . Anything you like, so long as you call by!'

She bit her lower lip, indecisive now.

He took a deep breath, bowed his head, put on a hangdog air and, staring hard at her, repeated in a very serious tone: 'Do come over.'

She rang the bell very lightly. When he came to open the door she had half turned as if ashamed at her boldness.

'Come on,' Florian said, politely taking her arm, 'don't be shy. There's no harm in popping over for breakfast with one's neighbour . . . This is my hovel. Make yourself at home. Sit down. No, not the chair, you'll be more comfortable there. Tea, coffee?'

'Tea would be fine, thanks.'

While he was busy in the kitchen she was looking round the room. There were books up to the ceiling. Plants, erotic paintings, musical instruments – a saxophone, a South American bandoneon, a transverse flute . . . A Japanese wood carving of a horse's head on the wall. On the floor lay Schubert scores, paperbacks, a solitary sock. A stuffed monkey grimaced in a corner, wrinkling up its nose. In the opposite corner there was an opaline vase of the Louis-Philippe period, the exact colour (this she was soon to notice) of Florian's own eyes. On a table rested a bottle of Château Haut-Brion 1973, three-quarters empty.

'What do you do?' she asked him.

He answered her from the kitchen but she did not catch what he said.

'What did you say?' she inquired.

'Oenologist,' he declared, returning with a tray stacked with tea-things, *petits fours* and assorted cakes. This he set down on a low table. 'And yourself?'

'Studying Classics.'

'With a view to teaching?'

'That's the idea, yes.'

He pulled a face.

'Teaching, God, what a pity!'

He sat beside her on the small settee. She had a pretty face and wore no make-up. Nice blue eyes and a friendly expression enhanced by her brown curls. Vivacious, open features. Her full, rounded mouth turned up at its corners in an impish grin. He liked her a lot.

He sniffed her scent and that pleased him also. Gulliver reared its head. This was how Nazulis liked women to be – natural, no make-up, no doubletalk. He leaned over her neck and indulged in a series of tiny inhalations. She recoiled momentarily, unused to being sniffed in this way.

'What's the matter?' she asked. 'Don't I smell nice?'

'You smell fine,' he murmured, leaning further across her.

He nuzzled forward and sniffing very precisely

21

progressed along her shoulder, moving on up to the neck, then her hair, which he barely brushed with his lips. She smelt of dry straw, the open air, good health. A natural scent of wholesome skin. She must be, he estimated, in her early twenties. Nazulis' nasal guesswork indicated that she probably came very easily, in uncomplicated fashion, first time out. It was anyhow clear that mind and body were in fine fettle. This was a healthy girl.

'Do you shave your armpits?' he asked brusquely.

'Why do you ask me that?' she said, uneasy.

'There are two sorts of women,' he explained. 'Those who shave their armpits and those who don't.'

She suppressed a giggle by pinching her nose.

'In the latter category,' he continued imperturbably, 'there are two sub-groups . . .'

She listened to him, chin on hand, unsure whether or not he was joking. But Nazulis was quite serious.

'One of these groups is comprised of those who simply let themselves go. They aren't bothered one way or another. And then there is the other group, the one which interests me. For them the hirsute oxter represents one element in their physical hyper-sensitivity and sophistication. Thus they look after the armpit, trimming its hair just a little, with scissors, to form a tiny silky island into which the nose enjoys delving during intercourse.'

He drank a cup of tea, replaced the cup, and went on.

'Do you remember how a few years back nearly all women plucked their eyebrows, leaving only a thin line above the eyes? Those lunar faces were a bit offputting, I always thought. Today there's been a big swing towards the New Hairiness: eyebrows are allowed to grow. Sometimes fashion displays glimmers of intelligence.'

While he was talking she stared at his hands, which were fluttering about like birds.

'Underarm hair,' he concluded, 'is sensuality to the ultimate degree.'

'I don't shave beneath my arms,' she whispered, smiling.

Delighted and appreciative, he pecked at her cheek, which was as velvety as a peach, then he refilled their cups with the passion-fruit scented blend he had bought in London. He wondered what colour her armpit-hair was and what shape the tufts took: rounded little islands or wedge-shaped thickets? Were they long or short, bristly or scratchy foliage?

'What's your name?' he asked her.

'Clémence,' she said.

'Florian Nazulis,' he announced, kissing her

just beneath the ear.

He relieved her gently of the cup she held and began stroking her hands – slender, distinctive, ringless fingers. Continuing to stroke her along her arm, whose delicate down he savoured, he reached the curve of her shoulder. It was smooth and warm, but the dressing gown hindered his caresses. He started undoing the buttons.

'No, no!' she protested.

'Yes, yes!' Gulliver insisted heavily, down below.

He leaned over and there was something of a struggle. Gulliver was in full cry. She was smiling and this made him want her all the more. Her half open dressing gown had revealed firm, round breasts whose pink nipples were now hard. He tried to undo the garment completely but Clémence was putting up some resistance. Holding her tightly by the wrists he succeeded in getting her onto her back along the settee. Then he wedged himself against her, lying full length on top of her, leg on leg, belly to belly, quimlet to Gulliver. 'Get on with it!' the latter urged him, his head battering at that delicious warm mound whose silky hair and disturbingly attractive scent were clearly evident through the material.

'You really are . . . passionate,' gasped Clémence.

Florian, atop her, was feeling too lecherous to

laugh or talk. His mouth found those sensual lips of hers and soon gave him her tongue; then both flickered, lingually conversing awhile. Her eyes were shut as she uttered a little moan of pleasure, a sort of slow, low recitative based on a single note. Gulliver continued his thrusts at the downy hillock. Florian's loins surged weightily and deliberately to and fro, and this relentless urgency gradually forced the adorable body beneath his own to part, open up to him. Gulliver, like a ploughshare, dived downward at the female furrow.

'Let's undress,' Florian breathed.

'Wait,' she said.

'I can't any longer,' he insisted.

'Wait, wait . . .'

The motion continued. The two bodies, linked yet separated by the barrier of material were coupling in an urgent frottage. The young woman's monotonous aria turned into a raucous panting deep in her throat.

'Ooohh . . .'

'Come on,' he repeated.

'Oh, oh, oh!' she burst out, astonished and overwhelmed by the orgasm which was swelling like a tidal wave.

Her body went rigid and she grabbed the man's shoulders violently. Head flung back, eyes closed, she let herself drown in sheer pleasure.

She had not even taken off all her clothes and there she was, coming already! Relaxed, looking happily flushed, she regained her breath. Florian was perturbed.

'What about me then?' he exclaimed.

'Another time,' she said. 'I have to leave now.'

She got up, kissed the young man perfunctorily, opened the door and disappeared.

For a long time he remained seated on the edge of the bed, head bowed, thinking. He didn't understand. He went across to the window. His beautiful neighbour had closed hers and drawn the curtains.

He put a record on the deck and began running the shower to maximum heat. Under the scalding jets his skin turned scarlet. Alfred Brendel meanwhile played Schubert's *Impromptus* with exquisite tenderness. Nazulis turned the tap towards blue and an icy spray covered him. He too began to turn blue and withstood the shock throughout the *Impromptu No 3 in G Flat*. When Brendel embarked on the first part of Opus 142, he turned the arrow to red again, almost suffocating in the steam while the pianist's dexterity, intimate and lyrical, recreated the despair of the composer of *Death and the Maiden*. The Prelude ended on an F Minor chord. He cut off the water for a moment and turned on the cold again, as Schubert calmly reaffirmed all the melancholy melody in that strange, inaccessible world of his.

Nazulis, skin glowing pink, emerged and donned a dressing gown. Gulliver, penitent and shrivelled, had been transformed into a ridiculous spigot whose sole, doleful function seemed to be that of purveyor of urine.

Revived by the vigorous shower, he seized the phone and dialled a number, whistling the *F Minor Impromptu* excruciatingly.

Somewhere in Paris, at the far end of the enchanted line, a woman answered.

'Hello?' a rather singsong voice replied.

'It's me,' Florian said. 'Has your husband gone?'

'Ah, good morning Lucie dear, how are you?' the voice then cooed.

Florian got the message.

'Call me back,' he said, before hanging up.

A few minutes later the phone rang, tickled into action from the other side of Paris by a dainty, delicate forefinger doing its sly work on the dial.

'Gorgeous one, it was quite impossible to get rid of him this morning. First he wanted to jump on me. Then he discovered he'd left behind a file . . . I thought he'd never go.'

'Can I see you?' asked Florian.

'Oh yes!'

'Now?'

'Oh yes!'
'I'm on my way.'
'Oh yes!'

When Florian set foot outside he stopped at once,
as if paralysed. He swayed from one foot to the
other, hovering and hesitating in the doorway of
his apartment block, expectant, yet unable to
plunge into the city's maelstrom. He stayed
where he was for a while, indecisive.

A bus passed, grimly grinding by in first gear,
and making the grey walls of the buildings bounce
back echoes. Opposite, level with the third floor,
a sander was scraping at the stonework, throwing
up a fine white dust which then sifted down a little
further on, ageing the unwary passers by. Further
away the noise of a demonstration was audible:
car horns blasting out slogans in morse. Something to do with somebody's resignation. In any
case the march went on repeating its particular
scansion of long and short blasts, while a heli-
copter covered the whole district with its rotor din.
In the neighbouring streets those other cars held up
by the demonstration played irate horn con-
certos.

Assailed as he was by noise, the various simul-
taneous commotions and that throng of assorted
aromas which seemed to strike him full in the face –

Florian could not make up his mind which way to turn. Then like a gust of breeze a woman swirled by, close enough to brush past him, and wafting a cloudlet of perfume in her wake. He followed hot on her heels, captivated by the scent of Miguchi, which brought back some delightful memories. She walked swiftly, swaying enticingly upon heels so high that her progress seemed a very marvel of equilibrium. Her legs were superb: trim ankles and slim yet muscular calves. He had not been able to see her face. Black hair gently bobbed in rhythm as she swept onward. Led, as it were, by the nose, Florian let himself be drawn along by the mingled odours of cypresses in the sun, pepper and nutmeg, which he recalled all too clearly: the beautiful Emilia from Turin had worn that very scent! But that was ancient history now: why dwell upon these Proustian madeleines, these olfactory titbits which titillated his nostrils so long after the event, remembrance of clings past? He half-turned abruptly and cannoned into yet another woman.

He lived in a smart part of Paris, filled with furriers, shoe-shops, boutiques and the like, and where the number of pretty women per square yard broke all records for the capital. She bestowed on him a dazzling smile as if the young man had actually caressed her. Her eyes were grey-blue and the vermilion lipstick she wore had smeared a fraction over her top teeth. Florian's hand instinctively shielded his eyes against the reflections flung from newly-cleaned plate-glass – the shop window of a particularly opulent and fashionable designer's HQ.

Florian took refuge in the doorway of a block of flats, trying to collect himself and keep calm. He then plunged into the crowd and made for the Métro, head down and hands jammed into his pockets. Just as he was crossing the Rue de Rennes he walked into a strong gust of *Diorissima*. He turned towards the perfume's purveyor but the blonde head had already vanished. Gritting his teeth he forced himself not to be diverted from his objectives, pedestrian crossing, Métro stairs, corridors . . . Borne on the wind were drifts of *Apple Blossom, Shocking You*, and whiffs from a man's shirt whose owner had bad BO. A group of yelling schoolchildren jostled him. He bent his head towards one of them and was reassured by the wholesome adolescent aroma thence exuded. Their teacher-in-charge looked at Florian suspiciously, but then the crocodile broke ranks and the hapless pedagogue had to rush to reassemble it.

Florian vaulted the Métro turnstile: this was one of his favourite exercises. One foot crashed into an empty beercan which clattered down the corridor. He retrieved it and tossed it assiduously into a litter bin. A little further on a tall, goodlooking violinist was busking, a saucerful of small change at his feet. He played the last few bars of an 18th century composition, emptied the saucer into his pocket and replaced it on the ground leaving a couple of one franc pieces in it. Then he slowly chinned his violin and thought for a while, an intent expression on his face. People funnelled down towards him, rushing for the train coming in with a dull roar to the platform below them. Florian stood expectantly in front of the busker, who winked at him before launching into Bach's *Partita for Solo Violin*.

The throng thinned again and the corridor was once again nearly deserted. The soloist played on as if in the concert hall. He must have had a Conservatoire training, ten years' practice at the least. Not a fault in phrasing, intonation or taste. The *Partita* with all its fugal and contrapuntal complexity unravelled effortlessly, with geo-metric precision . . . A circle of listeners had formed, enthralled by the virtuoso performance. The various musical paths of the *Partita* finally coverged in a resonant G Minor chord which reverberated throughout the corridor. The trav-ellers bestowed their largesse and departed. He got it right, thought Florian, dropping his biggest banknote, folded into eight, onto the plate. He avoided the musician's gaze, since being chari-

31

table invariably embarrassed him.

Mireille opened the door. She was wearing a mauve negligée. It exposed two round breasts which looked firm enough, for all their years of being fondled and sucked. Florian tilted back her head, she pulled down his, and they kissed lingeringly. She was a tall woman, blonde and somewhat marked by alcohol, sun and the general wear and tear of life, but still attractive. Mireille was a hot piece, an exceptional fuck. She would do it anywhere, any time. And probably with anyone, thought Florian with a trace of bitterness.

While he concentrated on devouring her mouth, Florian worked his right index finger into her slippery snatch, exploring that honeyed grotto. Mireille uttered little simian yelps.

Their favourite game together was playing monkeys. They would spend much time – when her husband and children permitted – aping gorillas, mimicking chimps and being baboon buffoons. They'd scratch their armpits, pull faces and emit jungle cries, leaping at and on each other in mock delousing rituals.

'Come on, you monkey, you,' said Mireille.

Florian followed her down the hallway,

absently sniffing his index finger: yes, all was well and healthy down below, on the evidence. Mireille was a scrupulously clean woman who visited her gynaecologist every couple of months, maybe even more often. (Florian wondered whether there was no ulterior motive in that; some additional, unacknowledged sensual excitement.) The kingsize marital bed was still unmade. Florian frowned.

'What's the matter darling?' asked Mireille.

'That smell of tobacco . . . Please open the window.'

'There you are, my apeman, that's it.'

'And do remove that ashtray . . . Why this mania they all have for sucking their cigarettes like deprived infants?'

'It's only mild tobacco, dearest . . .'

'Just as well, otherwise it really would be intolerable . . . Are the kids at school? OK, are they? Still behaving themselves?'

'Yes, darling. Quick, come on,' she said lying on the pink sheets.

'Listen . . . I'd rather you pulled the bedspread over if you don't mind. It's embarrassing to make love in a bed that's still warm. I can feel your husband's presence.'

'As you wish, my darling.'

After rearranging the bed she took off her nightdress and lay down on top of it.

'Come on,' she said to him, holding out her arms. 'Come on, my sweet monkey.'

Florian let himself be examined and turned over, and had his back scratched and ears nibbled. She flicked her little tongue briskly over a drowsy Gulliver.

'Just look at the little lollipop,' she crooned. 'My liquorice-stick, my dear little dolly, my sweet little bit of candy . . .'

She crammed in the tender morsel and began a subtle to and fro motion. At once Gulliver, delighted, started to stir.

'That's better,' mumbled Mireille as she darted her tongue-tip along the moist sinew. 'Ah the brute, the burglar, the slyboots, you naughty little beast you . . .'

'Mmmm,' said Florian, who was getting excited by now.

'Oh fuck me, fuck me quick!' cried Mireille, suddenly crouching on all fours and presenting him with her pink posterior.

'At last!' exclaimed Gulliver, plunging head-first into the blonde thicket.

'Oh yes, yes! Harder, more!' she was begging him.

Florian, standing over the bed, in the clutches and throes of love, abandoned himself to sensations.

'Yes, yes, oh, aaaaaahhh!' yelled Mireille, who

had by now lost every vestige of sophistication.

'Mmm?' he asked her.

'Oh yes, oh yes, fuck me harder! Again, more! Deeper!'

'Uh, huh, huh,' Nazulis panted.

'Split me, fill me, shove, fuck, more, more!'

'Ugh, ugh,' he groaned.

'Oh, I'm coming, I'm coming, I'm going to come, I'm coming . . .'

'Go on, go on,' a glassy-eyed Nazulis gasped through clenched teeth.

'I'm coming now . . . Yes, oh, I'm coming now, now, now, God how I'm coming, now, *now*!'

It was no bluff. Mireille being one of those women who get an enormous kick out of sex, which becomes all-engrossing, completely overpowering for them. She collapsed, demolished utterly, as if dead. Lying stretched out on the bed she resembled some great newly-felled African tree. They regained their breath and wallowed for a while in a contemplative calm.

From a deferential distance, Gulliver gazed at his master. A clock chimed. A lorry passed, gently rattling the windows.

Several minutes later they were at it again, this time in the missionary position. She was stammering 'My chimp, my ape, my sweet monkey,' with her hands pressed into the small of his back.

She had lifted her long legs aloft so he could penetrate her more deeply. At that moment the phone rang.

'Oh no,' she said wearily. 'Not now!'

'Don't answer,' said Nazulis, continuing to work away at her.

'Perhaps it's the school . . . I'm always worried something might happen to the children . . .'

'Don't worry,' he gasped.

Gulliver, turgid, imperious and sleek, grew ever redder and more taut, on the verge of his apoplectic apocalypse.

The ringing persisted. She lifted the receiver, while still connected to her Siamese twin, who would not be separated from her.

'Is that you?' she exclaimed. And then, her hand over the mouthpiece, she whispered: 'It's my husband.'

'Tell him he's disturbing us,' he puffed, continuing his seesaw.

'Yes, yes . . . I understand,' she was saying.

Finger up to her mouth, she was smiling at Florian, who took the hint. She covered the telephone again, whispering conspiratorially: 'He says he loves me and wants to fuck me . . .'

Nazulis, goaded – as a horse by a fly – began thrusting ever more vigorously and silently.

'Mmm . . . Mmm . . . Yes, darling . . . I understand.'

Suddenly Florian grabbed the receiver, winking at his lover, as if to say 'I won't give the game away', and with Gulliver in seventh heaven still buried deep inside her, he heard the nasal voice of the husband. That husband – the good father, worthy worker, and promising computer programmer who was still in love with his wife – the ideal husband, in fact, was expounding upon the hardship of being so far from his beloved little squirrel . . .

'Can you hear me all right?' inquired the uxorious voice.

'Mmm,' Nazulis answered, with a sort of upper-octave whine.

Then it was Mireille's turn to shake with a mischievous belly-laugh which sucked her lover into an irresistible ground-swell.

'You realize,' the husband went on, 'that I want you all the time, but I can't help it, as soon as I start thinking about your legs, those long blonde legs of yours, I get all randy . . . You know what I mean? Are you listening?'

'Mmm, mmm,' said Florian.

'My dear sweet feather duster, my tickly quim, you're always so hot and wet . . . Oh God, I'd like to come back home right now. How about you, are you in the mood for it? Go on, tell me.'

'Mmm, mmm,' Florian agreed.

'I'm really steaming now . . . I can just see your

furry snatch, as though I were right there beside you . . . Oh yes, I can see you all right!'

Nazulis winked at Mireille, who was now sitting astride him and fervently enjoying her belly-dance.

'. . . If you could see *me* now. There's a pile of files on my desk, stacked up to the ceiling. Fascinating stuff about our new subsidiary, for instance . . .'

'Mmm,' Florian responded, gripped by that muscular cunt which was sucking him in, snatching, squeezing him then bulging outward to force him back, before ingesting him ever more urgently. Gulliver was truly in its element.

'Well, you can bet I've forgotten about those bloody files, I'm thinking so hard about you! You're so close . . . I'm thinking about your arms and your hair . . . Then your mouth, your tongue, your teeth . . . your . . . ah Mireille my love, my dear little wife, I love you!'

'Mmm, mmm . . .' Florian repeated.

'Say something, though!' begged the voice.

Florian turned the receiver towards his lover.

'Ah yes, I sympathize, I really dooooo . . .' she at last gasped.

3

SANDRA – THE FUNDAMENTAL THESIS

Florian left his Number One lay (yes, fidelity in long-term relationships is a traditional virtue) late that morning. Mireille had to prepare the children's lunch while he was off to meet the ravishing Sandra, she of the gorgeous physique, who had so often posed nude for a variety of magazines. He scarcely knew her, but he could still clearly see her enticing adolescent body which had recently made the cover of *Him*.

He descended the staircase two steps at a time, sated and elated, inhaling from his fingers the fragrance of Mireille, that fresh and lingering scent of her recent pleasure.

There are those – and they usually qualify themselves as 'right-thinking people' – who would claim that Florian was a sex-maniac. The term would have given him a laugh or two. 'It's they who are the sex-maniacs', he'd maintain. 'They're the true obsessives of the sex war, the legions of killjoys, the anti-sexual mercenaries, always screaming 'Death to Sex!'

For Florian, lovemaking was no obsession but a constantly renewed pleasure which always changed and always began again, just like life itself.

Copulation calmed him, bestowing him with a joyous surge of energy. He and Gulliver existed in perfect harmony.

That had not always been the case. In his youth, Nazulis had wrestled with heavy bouts of conscience and angst. Those days, they tried to instil in him a sense of sin, a reaction of disgust against pleasure, an aversion to desire itself. The natural pulse and impulse of his uncomplicated libido had had to be misleadingly or mysteriously diverted or simply suppressed.

But he had come a long way since then, and had lost patience with neurotic priests, teachers and phony psychologists and other poisoners of the life-force. Gulliver, the modest, much maligned childish spigot had become a trusty companion-in-arms and an ever-ready confidant.

Florian had become perspicacious in the course of mocking established morality. He had learned to listen to the dictates of his naturally strong and healthy body. He knew how to understand and respond to his physical needs, to the inmost hints of his body's private language.

For example, sometimes his organism might say to him: 'Milk!' Then he would rush to buy a bottle of fresh milk. On other occasions his body would shout: 'Woman!' He would seize his rain-coat and charge down five flights of stairs to go out on the rampage.

Sometimes the physical demands were more precise: 'Blonde!' He'd riffle through his address book, hunting for those numbers marked with a yellow cross: Mireille, Florence, Sophie, Laurence, Carine. Then he'd pick up the phone. Or his body would transmit a more specific message: 'Brunette, on the hairy side!' He would thereupon loiter in the vicinity of the Portuguese Church in the Rue de la Convention. He knew that a plentiful supply of nice young chamber-maids and *au pairs* awaited him, shy and in-variably hirsute, even to the occasional mous-tache.

These physiological summonses drove Florian into a manic state of well-being, for what better can befall a man than a wave of desire and its satisfaction?

It could also happen that surfeit — too much food or excessive indulgence in wine and women — brought in its aftermath the need for a rest. Nazulis would then go on a 24-hour diet (herb tea or vegetable broth or total Gulliverian abstin-

41

ence) – time enough for his system to recuperate.

His body was not only sapient but also available. Whenever a new or unexpected pleasure presented itself, he would follow it and every inch of his physique would gleefully surrender to the sensation.

Florian, his body and Gulliver formed an inseparable trinity.

Thus it was that a few days earlier, strolling by the Square du Vert-Galant on the Ile de la Cité – the very heart of Paris – he had found himself in close proximity to a delectable creature. It was the early afternoon of a bright but mild day. At that hour the garden, surrounded by the waters of the Seine, was almost deserted apart from two or three *clochards* lounging on a patch of grass and sipping their rotgut.

Florian was not on the lookout for women. His body was well content after two early morning orgasms. Gulliver, snugly coiled in his cotton pouch, dozed tranquil. Meanwhile his master was contemplative, savouring the reflections of those ancient stones in the grey and yellow swirl of the Seine.

She was sitting on the actual prow of the islet

itself, propped against the stone parapet of the quay, gazing at the river. Her legs, slightly parted, allowed a glimpse of skimpy, skyblue-edged white panties, for her skirt had ridden up above her knees.

Nazulis's heart missed a beat when he saw this deliciously immodest display. She had glanced up and said 'Hello' in friendly fashion. He'd mumbled a sort of 'Good Afternoon' back, fascinated by her smooth tanned legs which, when one's gaze worked further up them, allowed a distinct and tantalizing glimpse of a downy mound that the tiny panties could not quite conceal. Eyes riveted upon this intercrural area currently being exhibited, Florian enjoyed a sublime moment of voyeurism. He was unable to utter a sound. The enthusiastic Gulliver at once twitched. And she had noticed, too, that sudden bulge through the thin trousers. Time stood still. Only the sparrows seemed to be carrying on as normal. His lips dry, Florian stood motionless, as if petrified and indeed resembling those aged stones everywhere about them, which had witnessed battles, revolutions, guillotined heads, and governments overthrown . . . She slowly ran her tongue over her lower lip and looked up at this silent man standing over her and staring at her with his blue eyes.

'Good God!' Florian murmured to himself.

She moved a fraction, shifting the position of her legs.

'Oh no,' he pleaded silently, 'don't you move, not yet, I want to look. Just stay as you are . . .'

But it was not the motion of closure. She had spread her thighs even wider and continued to stare back at him, smiling. Obviously she found this wild-haired man with the intense stare attractive. She had splayed out her right leg and tucked that same foot under her buttocks. Pulled taut by the change of position, the stretched cotton panties became even more revealing. He tried to discern the outline of the secret lips but the blonde thatch was too thickly furred for that.

He remained silent, standing there. Her eyes never left him. A serious expression had replaced her smile. She continued licking her lips, while her hand gently slid along her thigh towards her panties.

'Good God,' Florian repeated in fascination.

She inserted her middle finger past the embroidered hem of the garment and kept staring at him. Her mouth was half-open and traces of saliva glistened on her lips.

An American, surely. Her multi-coloured sneakers and checkered tee shirt, quite apart from her physiognomy, were not at all French. She was probably eighteen or nineteen. Her unabashed gaze quietly quizzed the young man while her finger worked on in slow, rhythmic rotations. The noise of water purling past over the stones of the Quai was clearly audible. The general hubbub of the city seemed a long way off. They were alone in the very centre of Paris, at the far end of this garden facing the Pont des Arts opposite, and further on, the Louvre.

She beckoned to him.

'Come on,' she said.

He drew very close to her.

'Isn't it just great here?' she opined in a distinct New York accent.

She laid her hand on Gulliver without ceasing to caress herself.

'Really good, huh?' she commented.

Then, still using her left hand she unbuttoned Florian's fly, fishing out a flushed and heated Gulliver. She bent her head, opened her mouth wide and swallowed. Immediately Florian felt a warm tongue lap him, back and forth in a steady tidelike rhythm. Her lips were clamped firmly around the jubilant Gulliver and her tongue was folded into a natural groove along which slid the tricorn tip of the tool and the underside of its shaft, thus procuring for Florian some wild sensations. He had grabbed the young girl's head with both hands. Her hair felt soft. The American girl was an expert in the tricky field of fellation. He soon felt the rising flood of orgasmic flux, welling up in an irresistible surge.

'Mmmm!' he murmured, closing his eyes as he sensed the imminent paroxysm.

'Wait!' she insisted, abruptly abandoning him.

Keeping him at arm's length she began to increase the speed of her own masturbation so that she too could reach a climax.

Frustrated by this sudden abandonment, Florian thrust Gulliver straight back into that wet, juicy mouth, thus obliging her to service him again.

'Wait!' she urged, pulling back to leave the electrified Gulliver stranded once again.

With furious self-absorption, her hand vibrating in an ever-accelerating momentum, she reached the very threshold of the spasm so long desired. She began breathing very heavily, then her head slumped and she came so violently that she was completely unaware of the man beside her – and now quite beside himself.

She regained her breath and treated Florian to a dazzling smile.

'That was wonderful!' she said.

Florian, his palms against the American girl's temples, pulled her face to the extended Gulliver. She began sucking at its head with tiny licks then, seizing the man's buttocks with both hands, she let herself be orally penetrated. Gulliver, sheathed to the hilt within this tender mouth, pulsed in rhythmic ecstasy . . .

Another day Florian had been sitting in the
starry night of a Champs-Elysées cinema, seeing
Barry Lyndon for the fourth time. On that
occasion too he had not been in a deprived state:
the previous night and the following morning had
been filled with embraces and delightful frolics.
Two women had succeeded each other in his bed,
and what was more, the evening brunette and the
morning blonde had been followed by a short
siesta at Mireille's full of stimulating exercise.

Body and mind at peace he had felt like seeing
Stanley Kubrick's masterpiece yet again. In order
to take his seat in the middle of a row he had
negotiated the obstacles of half a dozen rather
bony knees and finally found himself apologizing
to his immediate neighbour for treading on her
foot.

'Oh I'm terribly sorry . . . Excuse me.'

'That's all right,' she'd replied frostily.

She was an impassive if handsome woman,
with black hair pulled back in a businesslike style.
He settled himself comfortably, knees propped
against the seat in front and the nape of his neck
supported by the head-rest. The lights went down
and the film began. As soon as Handel's famous
Saraband resounded, with its martial and solemn
air, he had felt the pressure of an arm against his

own. He paid it no heed, again captivated by the scene where Barry seduces his cousin. The pressure became more urgent. He recognized the keen sensual signal and, moving his arm lightly towards his neighbour, responded to it. He loved those somewhat dubious situations in which desire takes advantage of darkness and anonymity to find its expression.

The female hand started softly exploring his arm and then found his own hand and was still. Barry Lyndon was serving his military apprenticeship. The adjoining hand led Florian's towards a warm and quivering thigh. Giovanni Paisiello's *Cavatina* accompanied the nonchalant decadence of powdered faces bent over the card tables. Nazulis loved the music. Completely absorbed in watching these eighteenth century duels, he started unzipping her jeans. His fingers infiltrated to find the warm nest, which his index and middle digits then delicately parted. She was sopping wet. He masturbated her to the strains of *The British Grenadiers*. Then, as the English army's guns opened up in a thunderous bombardment he felt her come. All this time the woman's head had remained motionless and utterly impassive.

The duel scene followed, orchestrated to the doleful beat of Handel's drums. She undid his fly-buttons and with her left hand jerked him off until he too came. She was even fastidious enough to wipe him with his handkerchief. Then, her eyes still fixed upon the screen, and indifferent to her neighbour, she watched the conclusion to the film. She left during the credits, respectable and anonymous to the end.

Yes, the three of them – Florian, his body and sturdy Gulliver – were in perfect harmony, making hay while the sun shone, and cheating death for as long as they could. Because, as Florian was well aware, it was by no means certain that there was paradise or even another world awaiting them. Florian had had plenty of time for reading and reflection on that particular score, not to mention considerable trials, errors and experience of life. One had to seize any moments of happiness here and now and in this world, before they disappeared.

In the movies, the streets of the city, the garden of the Vert-Galant or the vineyards of Bordeaux, on the Greek islands or wherever, Nazulis nosed out the various nooks and crannies of Paradise.

There are those who always lose the toss, as if fated. For his part he always called, and came up, tails.

If a young girl should decide to leave home in search of adventure, it was Florian she would run into outside the Gare Montparnasse. And guess who that delectable wife would meet upon the stairs of her apartment block, only moments after she had slammed the door in her estranged husband's face?

What about a certain February day on the ski run at Val d'Isère and those skis which came to a sudden halt right in front of our hero? Their owner was the sexiest, most sought-after Italian actress, by herself just for that particular day of days, without her 'constant companion', a macho type away shooting a movie at Cinecitta. She was alone, had beautiful blue-green eyes, and her famous arse was in the snow. Florian did not believe in God or destiny, but he was convinced some god or other was with him, Ah, that wonderful and cautious descent down the icy slope to the ski resort, her tiny hand firmly clasped in his as he guided her . . . And that come-hither look, the small curvaceous body which melted, writhed and clung . . . 'What memories for my old age!' Florian told himself. He'd also be able to tell his grandchildren a thing or two! 'Yes, my little lad, she was the Number One Box Office Star in Italy. Wonderful eyes she had. And I've led quite a life, laddie, I can tell you! Lots of wine, women and much else besides. I've enjoyed life to the full.'

Florian Nazulis was always ready for the unexpected bonus, the happy accident, the weird and wonderful encounter.

He was a true libertine.

Nazulis and Sandra were due to meet at the cocktail party celebrating the 1000th issue of *Gourmet* magazine. He knew that lovely body of hers from top to toe, and all its highways and byways too: firm, rounded bottom; curved slim thighs; little girl's breasts. Her anatomy held no secrets for him, nor for the readers of various pin-up and fashion mags, who would often find this nymphet-model plastered in all poses, in every degree of dress and wanton undress, across those glossy pages. There had also been that celebrated cover shot which had caused something of a scandal among all right-thinking burghers. In fact the capital had been covered with huge coloured billboards reproducing that same richly suggestive cover, and these turned every head. Parisian walls had never before sported such a provocative photo. Never had Woman so shamelessly exhibited herself. The Salvation Army itself was reduced to choosing between salvation or apoplexy. That was Sandra, all over!

At the party Nazulis spotted her immediately.

He elbowed his way towards her, rescuing her from the Managing Editor's inane witticisms, much to the young woman's relief, and dragged her over to a quieter corner. En route he had tucked a bottle of champagne under his left arm, filched from the tray of an aghast and beleaguered waiter. She worked her way rapidly through half a dozen glasses and he had soon had to find another bottle. He whispered all sorts of things into her ear and she kept dissolving into hysterical laughter. The guests turned in surprise, disconcerted by the raucous note that had intruded upon those serious topics under discussion in hushed tones. 'Crisis . . . Yes . . . You think he'll sell his shares? . . . No chance of election . . . No, definitely a new committee . . . Seven and a half per cent, no question about it . . .' Sandra continued laughing helplessly. Only one thing for it: Florian knew the most efficacious remedy. He pulled her towards him and started flirting. She let him do so, purring with pleasure then. Unfortunately they had to stop when Sandra's steady appeared, looking for her. As they left, she managed to tell Nazulis half-hiccuping and giggling into his ear: 'Come and pick me up Wednesday at the studio – you know where. We'll have lunch.'

The studio of the men's magazine in question occupied the entire top floor of a building on the Champs-Elysées. Its ceiling was dotted and hung with large spotlights which garishly illuminated a dais. On the latter were three straw huts, two palm trees and some sand. A huge backdrop blow-up of an azure sky and sea constituted the remainder of the decor.

Sandra was lying on the sand, nude, her arms flung out and legs wide apart, offering her private parts to the probing eye of a Nikon. The motor whirred and clicked on, taking shot after shot in quick succession.

'Great, fine, sensational,' the photographer intoned. 'Look up, higher, back, yes, again, turn your head a bit . . . no, right, that's it . . .' *Tchakaclick, tchakaclick*. 'Lift the knees, spread, wider for God's sake.' *Tchakaclick*. 'Now put your hand on it as if you're wanking . . . No, just one finger . . . Natural, be natural.' *Tchakaclick*. 'No it looks fake, do it properly, do it for real. Go on, that's it. Yes, fine . . .' *Tchakaclick, tchakaclick, tchakaclick*. 'Now turn and give us a bum, that's it darling . . . spread the cheeks . . . More, more . . . Let's see both holes . . . yes, right, fine . . . *Tchakaclick, tchakaclick . . .*,

On all fours, arse in air, Sandra managed to discern Florian silhouetted against the arc-lights. She winked in his direction. He gave her a discreet wave.

'What a job!' She confided, when she had dressed, giving him a tiny peck on the lips. 'What a crappy job. Where are we eating? Are you hungry? Do you think I'm sexy? Come on, let's go.'

In the lift she kissed him properly, deeply deploying her tongue. Florian was happy. He'd slid his hand under her flowered dress. She was not wearing a brassière. Her breasts were small and firm. Gulliver began to stir but the lift stopped and they had to get out.

They lunched at the Plougastel, in a nice quiet corner. The next door table was taken by a couple with thick Provençal accents. The man was a paunchy fifty year old rather reminiscent of the great Raimu. He wore a light grey suit brightened up considerably by a splendid scarlet and white tie – obviously brand new. She looked disapproving, her expression tight and menopausal as she repeated: 'Mind you don't spill it. You're bound to make a mess all over your nice tie and that'd be a shame . . .'

He continued eating in silence.

'Watch out or you'll spill it,' she would repeat whenever a waiter brought another course.

'I won't. I'm not about to spill anything,' he protested.

'I just sense it. I just know you'll make a mess *somehow*.'

54

After a while the man, utterly exasperated, bent low over his plate, took hold of his tie and dunked it comprehensively in his gravy.

'There's your mess, you were quite right,' he said, all but choking with rage, 'that's it. Another fine bloody mess I got you into!'

Florian and Sandra first ordered oysters and a Pouilly Ladoucette. They were hungry.

Quite soon they ordered two dozen more *Belons* and a second bottle. From time to time their hands and fingers would meet and tease. They were feeling content, knowing they would make love in due course. This prelude enchanted them.

'How old are you?' said Sandra.

'Thirty three.'

'Ugh, you're *old* . . .'

'Weell . . .' he said thoughtfully.

A waiter arrived to take their order. Beef and a Beaune.

'And how about you?' Florian asked. 'What age are you?'

'Twenty exactly.'

'You seem even younger, I thought you were about sixteen.'

'That's what everyone tells me. It's useful, sometimes. I can play the nymphet. I tell some guys I'm fourteen. It puts the wind up them, they're worried about my being under-age. To others, I say sixteen or eighteen. People I like, I tell them the truth – twenty.'

'What do you want more than anything in the world?' Florian inquired.

She thought for a moment and announced, 'Some roast beef.'

'No, don't put me on, tell me. What do you want more than anything?'

'Your cock.'

'Oh come on, seriously. I'd really like to know.'

She took hold of the Pouilly and refilled their glasses. 'I'd like all this to last,' she said, waving expansively, 'as long as possible.'

No longer was it a Nikon poised above her but a rubicund and swashbuckling Gulliver, rearing his pink head, ecstatically exploring that youthful, supple, plump body and its intimate aromas.

Lying naked on Florian's vast bed as if on a beach, with her arms and legs akimbo, Sandra, somewhat tipsy, was giving herself unreservedly, letting herself be penetrated again and again. Then she almost purred, sated. Florian suddenly passed out while making love to her and had begun snoring. She too gave way to sleep. Gulliver was also curled up taking a nap, cuddled snugly against the brownish downy mound pillowing his tip.

They all awoke, dazed and contented, after two hours deep and dreamless sleep. And began a celebratory romp. Sandra's warm and nimble tongue toyed with Gulliver. Florian, for his part, played with his tongue and lips upon the miniscule Gulliverette, that pretty cherry sweetmeat always so full of surprises.

Sandra's skin had a dark glowing tan.

'How do you get so brown?' asked Florian, wiping the lovely girl's elixir from his chin.

'In the West Indies. A modelling job. The photographer was goodlooking but he was absolutely impotent. He could only get an erection for a couple of seconds. And that was after working at it, I can tell you. 'Erection' isn't the right word for it either; despite everything I did, he just couldn't keep it hard and horizontal. Zap, it'd collapse, just like that. He never did succeed in putting it up me with the necessary member. Mind you, he compensated for that by all sorts of nice and effective alternatives, but for sex there's really nothing to replace the vital organ.'

'Do you often go on that sort of assignment?'

'Oh yes. The magazine likes my little arse. They sent me off to the Seychelles, the Bahamas, the Virgin Islands, India, the Philippines . . .'

'Always with the same photographer?'

'No, luckily. I've had Helmut, Roberto, Peter . . .'

'Do you always fuck them?'

'Nearly always. I like men. And sex. I don't go without.'

His eyes looking at the ceiling, head cradled in his hands, Nazulis was dreaming of distant isles.

'I like you a lot,' he said. 'You're a really . . .' He searched for the right word.

'Really what?' she asked him as she crouched to impale herself upon Gulliver's head.

'A girl who's really . . .'

He couldn't find the phrase he wanted. She began a motion up and down the swollen shaft which she could feel dilating within her.

'A really healthy girl,' he said.

When Sandra had left to continue her modelling session amid the coconut palms of the Champs-Elysées studio, Nazulis sat down at his desk and started writing.

For several months now he had embarked upon a weighty treatise concerning Bottoms. A quite serious, well-documented study, too. His thesis was fundamentally as follows: a woman's character revealed itself via her bottom and vice versa.

The researcher indicated how the shape of the female buttocks was the key to character analysis, and inversely, psyche. To this end, Nazulis had established a very full and detailed typology. There were groupings and sub-divisions of big bums, flat arses, perky podexes, jutting rumps, curved cans, dimpled cheeks, apple anuses, rosy rears, pinchable posteriors, droopy derrières, bony backsides and so on . . .

'The arse is a cultural phenomenon,' he wrote, 'which implies that it is by no means static but subject to change and development. As with all human organs, the arse changes according to use. Without erotic activity, it softens and spreads, the flesh becomes flabby, the muscles atrophy and it loses skin-tone, firmness and even colour.' ('None so vast as a respectable bum,' was one of his pet slogans. The oxymoron pleased him.)

'On the contrary,' he continued, 'libidinous activity and erotic athletics shape up the arse and give it suppleness and a streamlined appearance. Here are features which evolve over centuries, just like those of the human face . . .'

Nazulis supplied examples to which any unbiased observer could attest.

'There are sad bums and cheeky cheeks. Mischevious tails and dull dumplings. Sinewy and sinuous shit-holes, muscular meatballs, large lard-lumps, alas . . . Certainly too many slack, unhealthy sad mountains of adipose tissue and pitted with cellulite . . .'

In the Métro, Nazulis often amused himself by cataloguing the trim and the gross. He would compare their contours, assess the correct category, then move on to their owner's character. Sometimes he took notes. On other occasions he made a cautious approach, initiated a conversation. He frequently got short shrift, but now and then the woman might accompany him to a bar and, over a drink, the researcher would compare his notes with the psychology behind his interlocutor's line of chitchat. He would, in the most interesting cases, take his specimen back home with him for further, more detailed fieldwork. If he was particularly lucky, the woman might permit him to measure as well as pleasure her, and such statistics invariably enriched his dissertation.

One day, Nazulis told himself, he would receive the Nobel Prize for his pioneering work in this area.

The theory was not yet fully developed. There were, to be sure, exceptions. Wonderful women with wizened buttocks, or frail females with splendidly lunar, strapping posteriors. As with every exception, these only confirmed the general rule: each woman's character is inscribed on her arse.

After two or three hours' work, Florian visited his cellar and retrieved a bottle of Nuits St Georges 1969, which he brought to room temperature while going through his notes for the next day.

He put on a new tape in the Uher, checked its batteries and took the tiny capsule out of its case. This tiny microphone, as big as an aspirin, could adhere to any smooth surface. He tested for sound, fixing the capsule to the outside of one of the shutters. Everything was in order. He carefully replaced the machine and accessories into its container and poured a dash of burgundy, turning the glass and admiring the wine's fine, rich colour.

He raised the glass to his nose and delicately sniffed it, his eyes shut. '69 was definitely a mystical number, a miraculous year for burgundy after the disaster of '68. It was also the number of his flat in the Rue des Saints Pères; and, composed as it was of those interlocking curls, its fine numerical symmetry symbolized of course that other form of tasting which he so loved to practise.

The Nuits Saints Georges had such a delicious bouquet that Florian could barely suppress an exclamation of voluptuous surprise. For him it was similar to what he felt when appreciating a new and nude female body to which he was about to make love. 'The girl born the same year as this wine will be fifteen now,' he fantasised, letting the first droplets of the Premier Cru, called Clos des Forêts, slide across his tongue.

It was a full-blooded wine, quite lively for a burgundy, and though on the robust side, full of flavour. Florian smacked his lips and half-filled his glass. He held his glass up to the light, admiring the dark coloration of the liquid and trying to imagine its attendant twin or nymph. 'She'd have a sturdy physique, broad hips but firm arse, a steady yet soft look in her eyes, rounded breasts . . . Wouldn't shave her armpits, naturally . . . So young that she wouldn't yet have been brainwashed: no mania yet for keeping 'clean', i.e. depilated and deodorized . . . She'd still be a virgin and she'd have the scent of a young girl who revelled in the fresh air of Burgundy. Her hair (and pubis) would be luxuriant, sleek and black . . .'

He drank another mouthful, still dreaming about the girl, and letting the fine wine refresh his tongue.

The telephone rang. He rushed to cut off the call and leave the phone off the hook.

He did not want to be rung up. He wanted to be alone. For him the supreme happiness was to be able to choose his moments of solitude – not to have others choose to disrupt them.

He picked up the glass again, swirled the liquid within it, and continued examining its lustre against the light. He went on drinking, savouring the wine upon his tongue. Then he put on Schubert's *Sonata in A Major*. Alfred Cortot's version was a re-mastering and the original master had been rather crackly, but what an interpretation!

'Poor Schubert!' Nazulis thought. 'To compose those phrases, such musical intensity yet such simplicity, so every note seemed to strike the heart – he must have sweated blood! And he must have really loved women, that poor old ogling timid chap!'

Nazulis ran a bath, scattered a handful of *Youth Dew* salts and lowered himself luxuriously into the hot water, still holding his glass. The music had stopped. Only the trickle of the bath taps disturbed the silence.

After a moment he began wrinkling his nose with annoyance. 'No, that won't do at all,' he muttered angrily.

He got out hurriedly, dripping, and placed the precious glass of burgundy in the other room.

'That was damn stupid of me. What a thing to do!' he grumbled. He sank back into the water redolent of *Youth Dew*.

'Drowning Nuit Saint Georges in bath salts – what a bloody fool I am!'

4

CLÉMENCE AND THE CONFESSIONAL

At eight a.m. Gulliver woke his master. The
creature was straining at the leash, so swollen
that Nazulis was all but in pain.

'Hey, hold it, you're going crazy!' Florian
exclaimed. Gulliver bobbed assent, full of gusto.

Nazulis scratched his head as he hobbled over
to check his gadgets once more: tapes, mike,
wires, machine. All set.

She was there in her blue dressing gown, leaning over her blacony, smiling.

'Aha,' said the drowsy oenophile, 'you're
bright and early, aren't you?'

'Tea?' she suggested.

'Come over,' he said.

'Let me make it,' she announced on walking in,
'I'll sort it out.'

'All right, fine,' Florian said. 'The tea is on the . . .'

'I'll find it, don't worry.'

She returned with the tray. Florian had donned a dressing gown. Gulliver had relaxed somewhat. She put down the tray and without further ado knelt down in front of Florian, parted the garment and took the warm brute into her mouth.

'Hey, but . . .' the surprised Florian exclaimed.

She worked on with tongue and lips. 'Does that feel good?' she asked.

'You bet . . .' Florian said.

When Gulliver, now fully rigid once again, began to jerk and buck his head demandingly, she lay down on the bed.

'Undress,' Florian instructed her.

'No, wait. Kiss me, come on . . .'

Her breath smelt of peppermint. She had recently brushed her teeth with an American toothpaste — in all likelihood Crest. Her tongue darted with soft, swift, eager flicks around his. At times she would swallow his tongue ferociously before once again thrusting her own down his throat in a determined buccal onslaught.

'How about me?' Gulliver was protesting, beating his head against that melting pot still covered by the protective panties.

'Get undressed . . . I'll undress you then,'

Florian was insisting.

'No . . . wait, press against me, I like to feel you all hard against my stomach.'

She started moving her belly up and down, making rythmic undulations like a ship at sea, up and down, to and fro . . . He could feel her fill with salty fluids. But that damn gown, those quite unnecessary panties! He tried to rip them off. Gasping for breath, she defended herself, her body stiffening.

'Squeeze me,' she repeated. 'Rub against me.'

He made Gulliver lunge back and forth, ever harder, against her protected proffered loins. She herself was virtually on the brink of orgasm. She was breathing very heavily, clutching at his buttocks fiercely. 'She's going to come without me,' Florian thought and made a renewed effort to tear down her panties. He pulled their elastic which snapped but she still resisted, tense-jawed now. It was both struggle and embrace.

She delivered several culminating lunges before plummeting into climax, uttering a sort of strange, strangled gurgle which seemed to well up from somewhere deep in her larynx. Nazulis watched her regain her breath; she was close yet far away.

'God, that was good,' she smiled.

'How about me?' he asked petulantly.

Using her thumb and forefinger, she endeavoured to extricate a hair adhering to her tongue. She shrugged.

'How about me?' he repeated, he all but shrieked. 'Do you always get your kicks like that?'

'Like what?' she retorted.

'Swiss style.'

She shook her head, laughing now at him. Her hair flailed about her face, wafting that womanly odour, the incomparable scent of skin whose pores have recently oozed pleasure. Gulliver was giving Florian a hard time.

'I'm not on the pill,' she said.

'Oh,' he said worried. He got up and headed for the shower, Gulliver still stiff with unreleased tension.

'Come back,' she said.

He returned then, half hesitant.

'Lie down here,' she said, patting the bed beside her. Her tongue made about forty trips to and fro, from Gulliverian tip to scrotum. Very gently and deliberately at that.

'Oh, oh,' Florian began to gasp.

The tongue became more caressing, lingered longer, then turned rapid.

'Oh, oh! Ohhh . . . too much!' he groaned.

After a long teasing exploration, Clémence took the entire shaft in her hot mouth and waited.

'I can't take any more!' moaned Florian.

She remained motionless.

'Oh no . . . listen . . . Woouuu . . .'

She felt him dilate, contract and grow harder still, but she stayed absolutely immobile.

'Aaaouh!' he wailed, crazy with desire.

Then she sucked in her cheeks and bobbed back and forth again, forcing the rampant Gulliver to travel even further, before bursting at last with a white tide which pulsed and throbbed in nine steady spasms. Seconds after the ninth and final spurt, Nazulis, eyes still closed, took a deep breath, filling both lungs. He then exhaled equally deeply, emitting a voluptuous sigh of satisfaction.

'It might be a good thing if you did go on the pill,' he remarked.

'I don't often have sex,' she said.

'That makes twice in as many days.'

'Which is unusual for me.'

'I'd like to come in your arms, deep inside you,' he said.

'I'll start taking the pill next month, just for you,' she promised.

'You're a good neighbour,' he said, kissing her.

She stretched. One firm breast appeared as her dressing gown slipped open also exposing that delightful dark oxter patch which had given Nazulis such olfactory thrills. Her armpit tuft, seen from that angle, seemed quite long, its hair a deep beige.

'It's my turn: I'd like to suck you off too.'

'But you'd only want to fuck me afterwards, though,' she said.

'I promise not to.'

'I'm anti-abortion,' she added.

'I wouldn't fuck you afterwards.'

'Not even if I wanted you to? Not even if I begged you?'

'I promise. I'm against little accidents – having babies as a form of Russian roulette.'

She undressed and he finally saw her naked. She had a lithe, soft body, delightfully curvaceous, but not an ounce overweight. Her limbs were sleek and plump. Her breasts full and tilting slightly upwards, were crowned by hard, brown nipples. Under each arm there was that thick thatch, undergrowth enough to entrance the explorer. And beneath a wide yet flat stomach, lay a delta of fine foliage which he approached purring like a lovesick cat, drooling gluttonously.

He made her lie down with her legs apart and a pillow beneath her hips. Delta became promontory. The brown fleece, also raised aloft, opened into a pink, dripping ravine. A lukewarm liquid had trickled down it, past the arsehole, to form a little puddle upon the coverlet. 'Reminds one of shellfish', he thought. 'They all smell of the sea, mussels, clams, cockles, whelks or whatever . . .

A nice scent, I like it . . . Women are magical, marine delicacies . . .' He started lapping at the tiny bud that kept appearing and disappearing, tantalizing, elusive, yet real enough.

'A bit lower down,' breathed Clémence.

He had positioned his hands beneath his neighbour's buttocks. His tongue, plunging inside the aperture, worked to a regular, deliberate rhythm. She began breathing heavily through her nose, in a series of urgent inhalations and exhalations.

'Is that it, there?' he enquired.

'Yes, go on. Ah yes, right there, exactly like that. Don't stop.'

He enjoyed giving pleasure this way. His heart was beating hard and he was anticipating her paroxysm with a kind of awed impatience. To witness a woman's orgasm was a pure form of joy to him – the best illustration he knew of that injunction to love one another, so deformed and misrepresented by the Church. In that moment he did indeed love his neightbour, and with all the altruism of which he was capable. In this caress there was nothing for him: it was all hers, for her. And he thought only of her mounting pleasure, of how her excitement now inexorably increased. Mouth to that other mouth in all the heady intoxications of love's most secret kiss, he felt those preliminary throes which heralded her final

71

seismic seizure.

'Yes,' she gasped. 'Go on!'

At that moment there was no need to alter at all the pressure, rhythm or quality of the caress. It was the very instant of paradox, when the clitoris coyly retreats as if to avoid the supreme and imminent pleasure. A final tickle and the eruption would follow. Here was one of nature's own contradictions: the clitoris shrinking to sheathe itself, as if renouncing the extent of its bliss! Nazulis, who had loved many women, knew that at this crucial moment a man must never let up or let go, tracking the trickily reticent and burrowing bud . . .

'Ah yes, oh yes!' Clémence shouted.

Her whole body was rigid, overwhelmed by the onset and intensity of her ecstasy.

Florian felt the breakers of bliss surge over his tongue. Completely carried away, he had a violent temptation to climb on top of her, clutch her, and ram Gulliver home, deep into the dripping cleft. She even flung her legs up to receive the thrust. He burned to solder his body to hers in a blaze of bliss. But remembered his promise. And contented himself with sliding his tongue as far up the receptacle offered as possible, to the very lingual root.

Florian too was adamantly opposed to the use of abortion as a form of contraception.

'Do you have to go to work? the pretty neighbour asked him a while later.

The pair of them were lying naked and relaxed across the huge bed, just like good friends should. They weren't in love. The situation was quite straightforward. The love they had just experienced – that great wave of human warmth – they would have for any other man or woman, under the circumstances. They had indulged their mutual attraction. Clémence and Florian had not chosen each other, they had met by chance. They'd excited one another, nothing more. They weren't making plans to live together nor hearing violins. They liked each other a lot and that was it. (Sometimes, Florian would remind himself, there was nothing more miserable than a woman who flung her arms round your neck after a fuck and tried to keep them there for ever . . .)

'No,' Nazulis answered. 'I don't "have to" go to work. I work in my own time, whenever I choose. Every day I can hardly believe my good luck – no clocking in, no boss, no office routine.'

Clémence hung over the bed and took her dressing gown off the floor. She rummaged in its pockets.

'What are you looking for?' he asked her.

'Cigarettes.'

'Oh no, not that, please! Anything but that.'

'Are you allergic to tobacco?' she said.

'You could say that, yes.'

Nazulis did not need to smoke: he was not nerve-wracked enough for that. He felt no desire to inhale a futile and deceptive substance which would anyhow have ruined his sense of smell. He was happy to live the other side of the smoke curtain, aware of subtler aromas. Such abstention from that poison so freely available at every street corner meant that his tastebuds were spared, preserving their remarkable sensitivity.

'What's all this oenologist business involve?' Clémence asked, her forefinger tickling the drowsy Gulliver.

'I travel round the main winegrowing regions, the Burgundy and Bordeaux areas, the Loire and Rhône valleys and so on. Various vintages are obviously superior, certain years better than others – and I do the selecting for a number of French and foreign buyers. My function is to act as a sort of middleman-taster, the intermediary between the wine producers and the retailers.'

'Does it pay well?'

'Well enough, though I've no job security. Any day I might find myself out of work. Luckily I have a sideline which is also rather interesting: I write a monthly wine column for *Gourmet*, a gastronomic and travel magazine. This regular article means I have to get opinions and criticisms down in black and white, which otherwise I might never have formulated. A good exercise, since few things are harder than trying to classify and describe a wine. You have to find "correspondences", as that masterly word-connoisseur Baudelaire put it.'

Clémence listened to him as she toyed with the Gulliverian bush, teasing its hairs into tiny curls.

'Are you married?' she blurted out.

Florian looked at her warily.

'Why do you ask?'

'I don't know . . . I don't know you well. I'm trying to understand you, find out what makes you tick. You don't have to answer if you don't want to.'

She was experimenting with a pigtail effect, but the pubic hairs were too short to plait. So she placed a kiss on Gulliver's empurpled head, which no longer twitched.

'Marriage is the end of a couple,' Nazulis declared.

'Ah!' she said, almost as if assenting.

'It's the death of the couple, the institutionalization of love. It means social security, the suppression of adventure. Yes, it's the beginning of the end.'

'But there are successful marriages,' claimed the young woman, who had now found a comb and was carefully combing Gulliver's fur.

'How many? What percentage?' he demanded.

'I – I don't know.'

'Ten per cent. If that. The remainder, after the first six months of illusion, sink into mediocrity, boredom, frigidity, compromise and charades.'

'You're very harsh.'

'Marriage constitutes the biggest social con-trick going.'

'But . . .'

'It's a rat-trap, a fool's ambush.'

'Have you ever been married?' she inquired.

'Twice,' he replied. 'Each time for two years. The two experiences were worth having, so in that sense only, each was a success. Both times, as soon as things started going wrong, we separated. The greatest personal illusion and social hypocrisy is proclaiming "I'll always love you". There's no always. It's a snare. You only love once: that's true of most people. The individual evolves, everyone changes in his or her own way. The day inevitably comes when the two people involved are no longer complementary or mutually supportive. That's the day the couple should separate, quick, before things get even worse and they reach the final stage – hatred.'

'What about children, though?'

'Ah, children! That's the great argument in-variably produced by defenders of the institution of marriage.'

Clémence went on doodling with Florian's

golden fleece.

'One last word,' he persevered, 'and then I'll stop making speeches. We've better things to do than talk. Ouch, you're hurting! What was I saying?'

'The children.'

'The children, yes. Very important. It makes me sick when I see how they're brought up. What I want to say is this: happily separated parents are better for their children than parents who persist in living together despite not seeing eye to eye.'

Clémence let go of Nazulis's thatch, thoughtful now.

'Nothing's worse for children,' the oenologist went on, 'than being caught between their parents' mutual hate or indifference.'

'Right,' she agreed.

'I could tell you a thing or two yet to put you off marriage, but I don't want to play the wise old uncle. After all, people are free to do whatever they like, and to make their own cock-ups too.'

'I certainly don't plan to get married,' she affirmed.

'You never can tell. One fine day you might just get the urge – it's catching. You think you're starting with a clean slate and the odds are even. This time it's the real thing! You're starry-eyed as the ring slips on your finger. Then the weight drops and the trap snaps shut. There's no longer a way out. You're trapped, the pair of you, married!'

Florian waved both arms emphatically.

'Marriage, oh what an illusion! What an abominable insitution!'

The Church of St. Honoro-d'Elée, Place Victor Hugo, was one of the most fashionable in Paris's 16th *arrondissement*.

For a priest to be appointed to this particular parish signfied something of a rise in the religious hierarchy. Such a worthy would be working in a district with a God-fearing, conservative tradition. He would speedily adapt to this genteel environment and himself strive also to acquire an unctuous yet elegant style of speech.

The good *curés* of St. Honoro soon became (in the words of their flock) all too 'proper', very models of 'good taste', dispensing advice that was invariably 'discreet' or 'well-bred'.

At St. Honoro-d'Elée, everything reeked of the odour of sanctity.

Florian parked his car in front of the side entrance in Rue Mesnil. He glanced momentarily at the main door, where several nuns who smelt of

Marseilles soap were busily dislodging a peaceful spaniel asleep on the front steps. They also shooed away a flock of pigeons which fluttered off into the blue. Chiselled into the yellowish stone-work of the vaulting was an inscription that had faded to grey over the years. Nazulis deciphered it: D.O.M. SVB INVOCATIONE SANCTI HONORATI EPISCOPI. He blew a raspberry. The formula was, he thought, more than some-what stale. There had been all too many fine resounding phrases in Christian history . . . Above the Latin words the big bovine eye of a rosaceous plant seemed to stare over the Place Victor Hugo. Above it dangled the pendulum of the church clock, and that was surmounted by a bronze casing. To top the lot, a stone cross. So much for the entrance to St. Honoro-d'Elée.

Florian reached the porch. Just as he was pushing open the church door, he had second thoughts, turned round and dashed across to Lasavin's shop nearby.

There he knew he would find the finest choco-lates in Paris. 'Life's not at all bad,' he told himself as he selected an assortment of goodies, loading one of the tiny trays provided. Pockets bursting with sweets, he entered the church.

Along the silent aisles reverently shuffled the devout, sometimes overtaken by the whirring flurry of a soutane busily going about its business and characterized by muffled, scurrying steps.

A little old lady, moustached and muttering, approached a wrought-iron multiple candelabrum on which flickered holy candles of varying sizes (2, 5 or 10 francs' worth). She looked anxiously around her, first left then right, then vice versa and over her shoulder. She slipped some small change into the wooden moneybox and drew back again to make sure no one was looking. With a flourish she seized the largest candle and skewered it into place. Thirty days' indulgence. She hadn't wasted her time. Thirty days, a whole month's absolution! Oh no, she hadn't wasted her time in the least . . .

Florian extracted the mike from its case and entered the deserted confessional. A notice on the front door read: *Confessions from 15.00 to 17.00*.

The dark wooden cage ensured that you could only squeeze in upon your knees. Groping, he located the sides and corners of the cabin. He then took the capsule mike between thumb and forefinger and secured it high on the right hand side. There the sensitive apparatus could pick up every whisper.

Suddenly, with a sharp click the little communication hatch opened.

Florian had not heard the priest arrive. The latter was now silhouetted against the grille, mumbling in a voice so low that the young man could not tell whether he was talking French or Latin.

Ready to flee, Nazulis hesitated. The priest's voice was suddenly very loud and clear.

'Well, my son?' inquired this man of the cloth.

'Well, M. le *Curé*,' Florian echoed, not knowing what to say. I certainly haven't come to confess my sins, he thought, since God died years ago, and this infamous Church blighted my youth quite enough, what with all its mumbo-jumbo and lies . . .

'Well then, my son?'

Through the grating drifted the priest's aroma: he stank of boredom, along with an old man's odour of encrusted sperm and dried urine, of unclean underwear. His breath was heavy with constipation and tobacco. Florian had nothing against the poor sod personally, be it noted.

He decided to leave and made as if to do so before abruptly changing his mind. He leaned nearer the grille and stammered:

'I've masturbated five times today – no, six – in front of the image of the Virgin Mary. I found her exciting, you see. A virgin is always provocative, and what with her little blue veil . . . I fantasised that she hoisted her dress over her legs – she has really nice bare Mediterranean legs – and exposed her little knickers, the sort they used to wear in those days, made of transparent papyrus . . . It really got me hot . . .'

Silence. Nazulis the Blasphemer listened to the priest's breathing. It was the priest's wretched dogma, not the man himself, which Nazulis resented: the rubbish that had poisoned the best of his adolescence. They did me quite enough harm, he thought, for me to be entitled to a bit of revenge.

The silence continued interminably.

'Yes . . .' said the priest, softly.

'And then I raped a small girl, the day before yesterday, a girl walking through the school gates with her satchel under her arm. I offered her sweets. She got into my car and I took off for the suburbs. On some waste ground I raped and buggered her. Did everything. I beat her up until she didn't move any more. I took out my knife and cut her . . .'

'Hm,' said the *curé*.

'What? Did you say something?'

'I'm listening to you, my son.'

'Last week I poisoned my wife with arsenic. She was ill and running a fever. Flu. She'd become very ugly. Her face all pinched, bad breath and so on. I'll make you some tea, I told her. She drank her cup, staring at me with abnormally bright eyes, full of gratitude. You've just drunk arsenic, I told her calmly and she laughed feebly, thinking I was joking. I slapped her face and went out to pick up a whore. I took my time, and when I got back she was dead.'

The priest turned his face towards the grating.

'My son, don't you think you're laying it on a bit?'

'Not at all. There's worse to come. Three days ago I held up a . . .'

'Why do you take pleasure in telling me all this?' the man said, coolly adjusting his chasuble.

'That's what you're here for, isn't it? To listen to people's confessions. And what about my penance? You haven't given me a penance!'

'As penance, you must come back and confess your real sins . . .'

'I don't believe in sin!' Florian shouted furiously. 'What you call sin is a devilish invention created by moralists, cops and people like yourself, designed to turn people into sheep, and society into a huge flock for the greater profits of those masters you've always served. Army, Church and the Banks: there's your Holy Trinity.

'You ruined the best years of my youth with your ideas about so-called sins. You wrecked my childhood and now you louse up kids of the new generations. As well as adults naive enough to swallow your syrupy or threatening speeches and your pseudo-pieties. You're all the same – illusionists without real faith – because you don't even believe it yourselves . . .'

But the priest had left the box and was heading towards the sacristy, his shoulders hunched.

Nazulis made sure that the mike was securely fixed above his head. He came out of the confessional, left the church and got into his car. He switched on the recording apparatus, which was now set to pick up and record anything over a decibel rating of only ten. In other words, as soon as anyone began talking quietly or even whispering. Thereafter, the machine would automatically stop after 30 seconds of continuous silence. And of course the device also allowed for listening-in only. All one had to do was press a small green button.

This Nazulis now did. The amplifier transmitted only a vague hum, the generalized church noise comprised of murmured prayers, sniffles, coughs, stealthy footsteps, doors creaking, curtains swept aside. From time to time there would be a louder sound: the scrape of a chair across the stone flooring. For the time being the confessional was unoccupied.

He waited, enjoying his mastication of a peppermint chocolate. Then he chewed another, followed by a third.

At last the sound quality improved, due to the presence of someone entering the confessional box. A human body installed itself inside, knees against the wood, which creaked slightly. Florian waited for a while.

The click of the confessional door made him jump. There was the mumble (was it French or Latin?) of the priest, then a very young voice which became more distinct after various phlegmy clearings of the throat.

'I haven't been to confession since last Wednesday,' the little sinner launched forth. 'Since then I – well . . .'

'Well?' said the priest.

The child hesitated then gabbled his confession in a rush, without pausing for breath.

'I stole a box of nougat. I didn't do my maths homework. I said shit to my mother.'

'That's really sweet!' Florian exclaimed delightedly in the car. 'He's cute, this lad!'

And he crammed a *griotte* into his gizzard.

'Hum,' said the priest, 'that's not very good, not good at all. Anything else?'

'Um . . . nothing.'

The child was obviously wracking his brains – and quite sincerely too – in order to see what else might rank as a sin. But he had remembered and listed the lot, even before kneeling, so no, there was nothing in particular, nothing more.

'Really nothing else?' the cleric insisted.

'No, honestly,' replied the kid.

Florian was fuming. Was the old bugger going

to keep trying for his pound of flesh?

'No . . . impure thoughts?'

'No,' said the little boy, clearly confused by the priest's insinuations.

'No . . . fondling?'

What a shit, Florian seethed: I'll soon sort him out, and his cesspit too!

'No,' said the schoolboy, still quite unable to see what the confessor was driving at.

'How old are you, my young friend?'

'Ten, sir.'

'No impurities then, you're sure? As penance, you'll say ten Hail Marys.'

The kid, cockahoop at getting off so lightly, rushed off even before the absolutional claptrap had finished. The nougats had particularly worried him. It had been a big box and the shopkeeper hadn't seen a thing. Ten Hail Marys seemed a bargain, under the circumstances.

There followed the timorous snivelling of an elderly crone who had arrived late for 8 a.m. Mass that morning, having yielded to gluttony the previous day. Three helpings of cake, at that. The usual soothing reassurances, then a respectable citizen of fifty, the tight-arsed, tight-lipped type who had come to confess yet another wet-dream. This Holy Joe was succeeded by another sanctimonious female and a Portuguese maid who blamed herself for not working hard enough. Then there was a house-owner who confessed to exploiting her servant. ('But I pay all her Social Security for her, she costs me a lot . . .') After this microcosm of society Florian at last heard a voice which did not actually jar: what a wonderfully melodious voice it was, too! He turned up the volume control and listened.

The voice belonged to a young woman. After several venial peccadilloes she dared to get to the point, stammering slightly. For several days she could think of only one thing. It was obsessing and tormenting her. Nothing she did could dispel the thought, the picture of this . . . thing. Finally she had given in, and had taken to entering her bedroom, locking the door, lying down on the bed and pleasuring herself.

'This . . . thing, my child,' the priest said, 'which so obsesses you, what is it?'

She would not reply. Nazulis heard the noise of knees shifting uncomfortably against wooden planks.

'What is this thing?' the priest persisted.

A fraught silence.

'You can tell me everything, my child,' he snuffled.

The confessional was cracking apart, judging by the deafening racket of knees on wood. The priest's heavy breathing was also much in evidence.

'You must tell me everything, my dear child,' he insisted.

'Father . . .'

'This thing . . . Well?' he murmured unctuously.

She plucked up her courage.

'A prick!' she blurted out, bursting into sobs. 'I just think about it all the time, night and day. Being, um, penetrated, with deep thrusts of a prick!'

'Mmm,' said the priest.

'I know it's terrible, Father. What am I to do?' she sobbed.

'But what about your husband?'

'Oh *him* . . .'

Florian leaped out of the car and dashed into the church. As he charged towards the confessional he congratulated himself on having the knack of being in the right place at the right time. He reached the repentance shack just as she was emerging, her eyes red and with handkerchief to nose, on her way to kneel upon a suitable hassock.

Her penitential stance was the perfect position for posterior observation, and Nazulis was jubilant. Beneath her demure dark blue dress there was a superb, rounded arse – the sort of wind-breaker which, he was convinced, would work wonders in bed. Always assuming one knew how to go about it: i.e. getting it there in the first place!

Sitting three rows of chairs behind her, Nazulis composed his hands in a posture which a casual onlooker might have mistaken for one of piety pure and simple. Actually, a myriad lubricious pictures were racing through the young man's mind as he continued his contemplation.

He saw her get up, and himself rose to follow her.

She had a very slight limp. Each step she took she swayed a little to the right, with a barely noticeable awkwardness of that hip, though the movement in no way detracted from her manifest charms. On leaving the church she walked along Avenue Victor Hugo. He still had not seen her face to face. She took short, quick strides despite her limp. He loped along in pursuit.

Just as she was about to cross the street he caught up with her.

'Excuse me, Madame.'

Poised on the kerb as she was, she looked somewhat surprised and glanced askance at him as if unable to decide whether he was collecting, skirtchasing or conducting a market research survey.

She was very attractive and on the small side. A great quiff of blonde hair hid one of her hazel eyes as she turned her head. The other eye, however, was bright, intelligent and filled with curiosity.

'What do you want?'

'I was in the church just now.'

'And?' she asked.

'I was in the confessional with you. The other side.'

A moment of hesitation. The 82 bus passed, punishing its first gear as usual.

'So?' she said drily as the bus moved on.

He stood right in front of her and looked her straight in the eye.

'I heard everything.'

She turned pale. Her mouth opened and closed noiselessly like that of a stranded fish. She reeled, tried to regain control of herself, but promptly blushed a deep scarlet.

'Don't worry, Madame,' he said in a jovial tone, taking her arm. 'Nothing to get steamed up about. Your so-called sins are trivial enough – the odd fantasy, some mild masturbation, dreams of a big dick . . .'

'Oh, please!' she gasped.

'Come on then!' he blithely urged her. 'Don't be upset, my dear little lady. Fantasies are only natural, after all. And quite healthy. A big hard prick, eh? No, no, don't argue, don't worry: relax, come on. Calm down.'

'Where are you taking me?' she all but whispered.

'My place,' he said.

He bent over her for a moment and surreptitiously took a couple of sniffs. Guerlain's *L'Heure Bleue*: he liked that one. A mellow, flowery, spicy scent.

'Your house! Oh no. Out of the question,' she protested.

She was pleading with him, he could see it in her eyes. Her pretty face, still flushed, was lightly made-up: a daytime foundation cream with an apricot aroma he had distinguished at once; a touch of Rimmel around the eyes; a trace of pink eye-shadow.

'No no, I beg you, I – ' she was repeating.

'Come along,' he said, smiling broadly.

He looked as if butter wouldn't melt in his mouth: a young man of neat yet distinctive appearance, with an attractive and open face, obviously honest. He was dressed in British style, what was more – silk scarf (doubtless from Hermès) and dark green tweed jacket with leather elbow patches. Yes, Florian was clearly well-dressed, well-bred and well-educated. Hadn't she met him at St. Honoro-d'Elée, after all?

'No, no,' she went on protesting feebly, but she let herself be walked to the car.

He opened the door for her, carefully stashed the recording equipment and turned the starter. All aboard for the bed of pleasure!

'It's not possible, just not possible,' she repeated.

Her voice had a definitely upper-class intonation but was lilting enough to delight the ear. God how he wanted to make her yell! How she would scream with pleasure at the thrusts of that long-desired prick . . .

Florian drove well, smiling. He placed a hand on her warm thigh and she jumped.

'Come on, don't be childish – you're a big girl now. The time has come to live like an adult, according to your desires . . . 'Deep thrusts of a prick' was how you expressed it.'

'Stop it!' she sobbed. 'I'm ashamed . . .'

He stopped the car at the far end of the avenue and took her in his arms like a father cajoling a young daughter, stroking her hair and holding a handkerchief to her nose.

'Don't cry any more . . .'

'I'm so ashamed . . .'

'Nothing to be ashamed of. Though it's time you became a free, independent individual. They taught you to reject desires, repress your feelings, mortify yourself. You have to sweep away such crap. Relax, for God's sake!'

'But . . .'

'Fantasies like the ones you mentioned are *good*! That I promise you.'

'Stop this! I want to go back home . . .'

He put his arm around her, stroked her cheek and brushed away a tear. Her big eyes were staring at him with a lost child's expression. He tilted back her chin and gently kissed her lips. She no longer protested. Her eyes closed. She did not fully open her mouth but then she didn't close it either. He massaged her a little before sliding a hand under the top of her dress. He could feel her brassière with his fingertips. A sad mistake, at her age, he thought . . . Then he cupped her whole breast with his hand. She uttered a tiny moan. He began ferreting around her belt and undid the dress. She did protest at that, and struggled a bit. He persisted and managed to insert two fingers inside her panties. The hair they felt was soft, warm, silky. She struggled again, but he slid one finger against her vulva. She was wet, absolutely sodden with desire. Which illustrated the Christian neurosis, Florian reflected: the mind saying No while the body said Yes.

'Oooh,' she said, surprised to feel such pleasure rise in herself, as successive waves of emotion threatened to overwhelm her.

She sprawled all loose and relaxed across the

confined space of the car seat, her legs wide apart, as if his for the asking. He continued caressing her, and his finger worked inexorably to and fro, prompting a series of puppyish yelps from the young woman.

Then he took one of her slim hands and laid it on Gulliver. The latter had been straining under Florian's trousers for what had seemed an interminable time.

'Dear God . . .' she gasped, amazed at the firmly cylindrical bulge.

'That's what you wanted, wasn't it?'

'Oh . . . my goodness . . . oh . . .' she repeated in fascination.

'That's what you needed, wasn't it?' he remarked, his tone now slightly brutal, though she did not seem to notice or care.

'Oh yes, yes,' she murmured.

'Let's go, then,' he said, turning the starter key.

While he was driving her fingertips shyly stroked that 'thing' of her dreams and fantasies.

'You can do that harder, you know. It won't break,' he commented.

She did not dare. With a swift movement he unzipped and the animal's head popped out of its pouch, glistening and shamelessly scarlet.

Her eyes goggled in astonishment. She was temporarily speechless.

Had she never examined her husband's (Lilliputian?) Gulliver close to? It seemed as though she were discovering the prime male organ for the very first time.

The passengers in a car beside them at the red light were craning over, all agape. Florian burst out laughing and waved, half friendly, half mocking, as the lights changed to green.

They travelled along the Boulevard Saint-Germain and the Rue de Rennes, to Place Saint-Sulpice, the heart of the 6th *arrondissement*, full of trees and strolling pedestrians. It was a cheerful and lively scene, despite the preponderance of creepy little religious shops where old folks from the provinces could buy rosaries, missals, and assorted edifying and devotional paraphernalia.

On this square dominated by the ugliest, most lumbering church in Paris, a veritable sacred bunker, children were roller-skating round the monumental fountain which sprinkled frothy sprays of water over the stony shoulders of Fénélon, Bishop of Cambrai; Bossuet, Bishop of Meaux; Eflechier, Bishop of Nimes, and Manillon, Bishop of Clermont. Four bland old boys sitting unperturbed amid the deluge, guarded by four roaring lions. Four worthies, well and truly out of it, far removed from the world and its realities – kids, roller-skates, birdsong and lovers on benches.

Florian parked the car beneath a plane tree. Her head was still lowered, she was still staring at that dream pistol of hers, on whose rubescent tip twinkled a jovial teardrop of clear liquid.

'Desire,' he said. 'I get wet too.'

She dabbed it with one finger to collect a drop of fluid and raised the finger to her nose. Odourless. Next she tested it with her tongue.

'Sweetish,' she said.

He turned towards the young woman. Her expression had about it a beautific, expectant intentness.

'I want you so much,' he said.

'I want you too. I've never felt quite this way before,' she said, running her hand through Florian's hair.

'Have you ever been unfaithful to your husband?' he asked, playing with her platinum engagement ring set with diamonds.

'Never,' she said.

'Did you have any other men before him?'

'Not intimately. One or two flirtations at the most.'

'What do you mean by "flirtations"?'

'Amusements. Nothing below the belt.'

'So you were a virgin when you married?'

'Yes.'

'Incredible!' he exclaimed. 'So it still happens,

even in 1985! This bloody religion really does poison people's minds, to this day. And what does your husband do?'

'He's quite high up in the Ministry of Defence.' Florian suppressed a grimace.

'Does he love you?'

'Sort of.'

'What does that mean, sort of?'

'He's certainly very fond of me. He's a thoughtful, affectionate person.'

'Does he make love to you often?'

'Once or twice a week.'

'What?'

'Once or twice . . .'

'I heard you all right. It's dreadful – a woman like you, beautiful, young, sexy . . . Once or twice . . . What a waste! What a sod he must be! How sad!'

She snuggled close to him, so near and so lonely. She was looking at him with those distinctive pale eyes. All at once Florian felt like weeping, like having a damn good cry. The world was full of strange anomalies quite beyond his comprehension. Sometimes he no longer understood anything.

He took her hand and pressed it to his lips, sensing that what was happening to them in that transient moment was far beyond desire. Between them, between their spoken or unspoken words, between the lines, there was something invisible. Quite simply, it was love. A moment of love without calculation or conventions, without past or future. Absolutely gratuitous as only real love can be. He sought nothing from her; she had her life and he had his. Their paths had crossed. Perhaps they might never see each other again.

'What's your name?' she asked.

'Florian,' he said.

'Fancy,' she said, 'our names are almost the same. Mine's Florence.'

She laid her head on his shoulder. They stared up at the pinnacles of the church of Saint-Sulpice, those formidable and lofty bastions.

'Moments like these make life worth living,' said Florian. Certainly there was desire, for they both knew that they were soon going to fling themselves on to a bed in a few minutes, and be shaken by the Great Earthquake, but just then they were beyond desire. Love itself goes beyond desire. Gulliver too had relaxed, as if instinctively understanding that love goes beyond sex. Indeed he waited confidently in his nook, knowing all too well that the young master never passed up an opportunity. Just for now, the master himself was in love. It wasn't the time for frisking and frolics. Gulliver waited.

Ah, they were getting out! he realised happily after a period of silence. A rush of excitement filled Gulliver, which reared readily at the thought of plunging headfirst into that wonderful well so redolent of womanly desire.

Gulliver all but crackled with erectile electricity.

5

FLORENCE AND THE MIRACLE

Florian was right. Florence revealed herself to be a fantastic lover.

How, though, was it possible to prove so adept at amatory arts after so little practice? She must somehow have learned from all those amorous orgies she had never actually experienced, imaginatively recreating every sexual encounter hitherto forbidden.

She certainly knew how to compensate for her inexperience and lack of confidence.

'Shall we get into bed?' she asked her abductor timidly.

'We'll get on to the bed. I want to look you over from head to foot, my beauty.'

She started to undress methodically, like a schoolgirl, folding her dress with care before laying it across a chair.

'Wait,' he told her. 'I'm the one who'll take off your clothes.'

She allowed him to do so, showing traces of embarrassment, unused as she was to these sexual rituals.

'Am I hurting your leg?' he asked as he was removing her white silk petticoat.

'No of course not. Why?'

'I noticed you were limping slightly. Did you have a ski accident?'

'No, it's the sciatic nerve in my hip . . . I'm not really sure, but I've been in pain for two or three months. It hurts when I walk. I've seen several specialists, to no avail.'

'Doctors, well yes . . .' Florian said with a sceptical dismissive frown, continuing to slide a pair of tiny embroidered cotton panties down her long, slender legs.

As soon as she was naked in his arms, trembling and quivering with desire, Florian slipped down so that his head was poised between her legs, ready to render the initial homage, for play and foreplay, of the oral embrace.

'No,' she gasped. 'Do it quickly please, inside me, quick.'

She parted her legs, raised her knees a little and held out her arms to him. Her slim, warm body still had the remnants of last summer's suntan. Two small firm breasts tilted in youthful pride. Her legs were trembling.

He gazed at her with momentary apprehension.

She wore an expression of such intensity, such concentrated passion – a crazy look, in fact – that he was dumbfounded, motionless. She grabbed his shoulders with immense strength, and he felt her nails sink into his back like an eagle's talons gripping its prey. She pulled him abruptly onto her stomach and was penetrated at a stroke.

Only then did she relax. Her hands released their grip and her muscles too unclenched. Her eyes lost their demented stare.

She undulated her belly in a slow, supple grind, linked now to her lover's own loins. Propped somewhat uncomfortably on his elbows, he thrust downward at her and could thus observe her too, fascinated by her absorption, by the fervour of her lovemaking. He had fucked many women (he was one of the most notorious womanisers in Paris), but he had never yet witnessed such ardour during intercourse.

'It's even better than I dreamed,' she murmured.

'What would you like now?' he asked. 'What would you like me to do?'

'I used to have one particular fantasy. I'll show you what I mean.'

She uncoupled and knelt on the bed, her head bent, leaning forward like an animal on all fours.

'Like this,' she said.

Admiring the superb curvaceous rump thus

raised and proffered to him, Florian let Gulliver's round tip truffle at the moist mound.

'Strike as hard as you can,' she said.

Florian hesitated for a second. What did she mean by the odd verb 'strike'? Spanking those lovely, plump cheeks with whip or cane, crop or switch? Beating of buttocks till they bled and she came? He fervently hoped it was not the case and she didn't get her kicks that way. He'd never been one for SM games. He liked to stroke not strike. Loved love, not violence.

'You want me to beat you?' he inquired anxiously.

'No, no. Not strike *me*, just to go deep, drive into me hard, as hard as you can, into me from behind.'

Florian had further misgivings: what did she mean by that last phrase? Did she want him to bugger her? Why not? he asked himself. It really wasn't his speciality, so to speak, nor did he rate sodomy as a more pleasurable option than any other (though there were plenty of anally-fixated characters who would disagree), but if that was her desire he was ready to satsify it.

He pressed his finger against the alternative entrance and felt the taut elasticity of the puckered membrane.

'It needs some lubrication,' he suggested, 'otherwise it's not too easy. Might be painful.'

He put out his tongue and tenderly and conscientiously accomplished the manoeuvre dubbed by erotologists *feuille de rose*.

She began laughing and her whole bottom shook. The sight was irresistibly provocative.

'When I said "from behind",' she explained, 'I only meant the position, not *that*.'

'I see,' said Florian, with relief.

There were no further misunderstandings or reciprocal agreements. Gulliver to the fore, he penetrated her by the more customary highway, which was sleek and hot. His poker stoked her ever more vigorously.

'Aaaaaoooooaaah!' she was wailing interminably, her mouth jammed against the mattress.

Every time he sensed her nearing climax, he accelerated his rhythm and dug deep between those firm cheeks which slapped against the skin of his inner thighs. When he felt her beginning to come, he pounded away faster still, like an express train going flat out. She was coming. He could feel orgasmic contractions around Gulliver's glans, and that telltale sprinkling increase of moisture. He slowed pace accordingly and counted aloud: 'Four!'

Then he recommenced, panting and sweating like a woodcutter, and counted out a new series of strokes, concentrating upon a mass of foliage flailing in a high wind before crashing spectacularly to earth.

'Five!'

'How can you keep hard,' she managed to gasp between two loud groans, 'and stay like that for so long? My husband goes soft straight afterwards.'

'That way he's got time to spare for his weapons and wargames . . .'

Florian resumed his pit sawyer's regular rhythm. 'Six!'

'Why are you counting?' she asked, her face still pressed into the mattress.

'Hoarding pleasures . . . Woodcutter's pride . . . Trying for the record . . . I don't know.'

'I can't take any more,' she moaned, against the sheet, her voice muffled.

'Wait! Go on, go on!'

He worked on, driven by obscure forces of which he was merely the instrument and Gulliver but the instrument of an instrument. In – out, in – out, more, more, deeper . . .

'Seven!'

'Stop, Florian, I can't go on . . .'

They collapsed in a heap, breathless, sweat-drenched and drunk on orgasms.

'How can people who don't make love exist?'

said Florence, her toes toying with Gulliver.

'I often wonder myself,' Florian said.

'One feels so at ease. You seem to understand things better, with heightened perception. The world looks brighter.'

'The world belongs to those who fuck,' he affirmed.

'But how do you manage to stay hard for so long?' she asked.

'Whenever I feel myself about to come, I hold back. I slow the rhythm, stop or wait. There's a sort of friendly rivalry between Gulliver and myself; he wants to shoot off and I'm trying to restrain him.'

'Gulliver?' she said.

'My best friend, loyal companion and inspirer of my keenest pleasures . . . Down there,' he pointed.

'Ah, that – "the thing"!'

'Yes,' said Florian. 'Whenever I keep him well under control, so the old rascal's straining at the leash, in fact, I can start up again in a flash. The pleasure is more overwhelming, far greater if orgasm is delayed. Desire increases in proportion to the delay in satisfaction. The keenest ecstasy is that of the sharpest desire. The big mistake in lovemaking is coming when the desire is too weak. Most neuroses stem from that. Very often people feel dissatsified afterwards because they haven't given their desire enough time to grow. They come too soon, too lightly, and they are discontent.'

'So you haven't come yet?'

'Not yet, no.'

'And that's why you were able to make love for so long, so much?'

'Yes.'

'I've never had so many orgasms, one after the other. It was incredible. It was . . .'

'My method,' he said.

She gazed at him in admiration, bright-eyed. He wasn't being vain about this ability of his which so often astonished women. Prolonging the enjoyment was quite natural for him, tension adding a necessary, voluptuous edge to pleasure's urge.

'But you must want to come so dreadfully, don't you, after holding back for so long?'

'Yes.'

'Do you know what I'd really like to do?'

'No,' he said. 'I don't.'

His lips were teasing at the down on Florence's nape, just where the hairline proper begins.

'I want to do everything I haven't done so far.'

'Tell me then.'

'My husband doesn't think I'm interested in certain things.'

'The turd,' said Florian.

'He's only ever had me in the missionary position, mechanically and too fast.'

'Doesn't surprise me.'

'I'd like . . .'

'Anything you want,' he promised.

'It's sort of greedy of me but . . .'

She hesitated.

'It might seem odd to you,' she said.

'I've done plenty of fairly odd things myself, in this field,' he admitted.

'I . . . I . . .'

She couldn't bring herself to put it into words.

'Look, get one thing straight,' Florian said. Then he continued, very slowly and deliberately: 'Everything is permitted.'

Finally she plucked up enough courage to blurt out:

'I'd like to make you come. With my mouth.'

'A delightful wheeze,' Nazulis said approvingly.

'I'm not sure I'll be very good at it, but I'd like to try.'

'It's soon learned,' Florian said.

'But I've never . . .'

'I'm sure you've a talent for it. The main thing is, be very careful with the teeth. Use only the lips – the lip muscles are ideal for the purpose – and the tongue.'

He lay on his back, tucked a cushion comfortably under his head, and let her get on with it.

'Like this?' she asked.

Over-eager to perform well, she accelerated the osculation, almost knocking Gulliver flat in her zealous onslaught.

'No, that's not it,' Florian informed her. 'Too abrupt. You have to go slower, start gently, rhythmically, sensually . . .'

She gripped the Gulliver tube in her right hand and lapped with her tongue in circular sweeps around the violet head.

'That's fine!' Florian exclaimed. 'Go on. Oh yes, oh yes, oh, you've got the knack all right . . .'

Giving her instincts their head, Florence in a series of serious licks moistened the bulbous tip which swelled and hardened, about to explode.

'Oh yes! Yes, yes!' muttered Florian, who had almost taken leave of his senses.

He was seeing fiery abysses, sulphurous craters where incandescent lava boiled. Molten stones shot upwards like rockets, spattering the night with comet-trails . . .

She had engulfed the glans gently, taking care it did not touch her teeth, and was moving it to and fro between her lips.

'Oh, oh, oh,' he murmured. 'Listen, when I come, don't stop that movement, keep me in your mouth to the end.'

The doorbell rang. It made Florence jump.

'Don't worry,' he gasped. 'A salesman or a survey or something – who cares . . . Go on.'

She continued her embrace, lips and tongue attentive, assiduously increasing his pleasure.

'Wwwwwaaaaoooouuuh . . .' Florian moaned.

At the crater's rim, vast showers of sparks burst, scattering skywards in an enormous firework display. The surface of the crater, lashed by a storm originating from the very depths of the planet, flung gouts of earth, lava and white-hot metals into space.

She felt the engorged organ dilate still more until it was burning hot and rock hard.

Nazulis, fists clenched like an angry baby, eyes closed, muscles contracting, remained motionless.

She received the first spurt on her tongue, hot and sticky, then a second. Then it was her turn to count, as his spasms succeeded one another. Three, four, five, six, seven . . . There, she told herself, we're even. But an eighth jet swamped her throat and she waited for the next. Nothing more – that was it.

'Ye Gods,' he said. 'You did that like an expert.'

'I've been wanting to try it for so long,' she said contentedly, curling up in the young man's arms.

For some time they did not say a word, like spaced-out junkies whose heads are full of private clouds and lights.

He was flying above the dark green, endless tresses of the Amazon forests. Then there was the sea, that tranquil expanse of bluish-white reflections . . . A dove flapped its wings, fluttering momentarily in the azure sky and tracked by the inner eye of a bedazzled Florian. Florence had placed her hand over the drowsing Gulliver.

'Moments like these, too, make life worth living,' Florian murmured.

The doorbell rang again. Nazulis pulled on a dressing gown and in a split second – for he had the feeling of walking on air – had opened the door.

'Awaken!' chorused two characters, each clad in blue caps with earflaps and chinstraps. These females were brandishing booklets on which was depicted a bilious-looking sun.

'I beg your pardon,' he said, rubbing his eyes.

'Wake up, wake up!' gabbled both these girls of indeterminate age, their tone joyously hectoring as they waved their brochures under Florian's nose.

Both wore khaki army-surplus tops and dark red, nearly heel-length skirts. Clumping ethnic sandals shod their large white feet, while their faces, brightened only by occasional flashes of yellow teeth, were a pasty hue.

'God is with you!' they announced reassuringly. 'He can help. Business success. Shine in society. Overcome shyness. Making money. God is with you! Wake up!'

'You've got some nerve, I must admit,' Nazulis said crossly.

'God is everywhere. Awake . . .'

'All right, I heard you the first time,' he said. 'How much for all this bumf of yours?'

'You can give whatever you like,' they said in unison.

'Whatever I like,' he repeated, scratching one armpit and then the other and automatically sniffing his fingers. 'Whatever I like?'

'That's right,' they confirmed. 'A hundred francs, for instance.'

'Or maybe more,' suggested one of them eagerly, with an avid yellow smirk.

'Or maybe more . . .' Florian echoed. He suddenly adopted a regretful look.

'Yes?' they said in a tone which was the prelude to all sorts of special bargains.

'There's a threefold problem,' he said.

'Ah – a threefold problem?'

Their eyes became shifty and they shuffled about uneasily.

'Yes. This is it. 1. I'm quite awake. 2. God is

dead. 3. You're beginning to cramp my bollocks.'

'Oh!' They exclaimed in horror. Their eyes were goggling now, their mouths pursed tight as chickens' arses.

'Don't you believe me? Look!' he shouted, pulling his dressing gown wide apart. 'See what you're doing to my balls?!'

They took off down the staircase as if pursued by the Furies, losing various pamphlets en route. These fell open to reveal brash title pages: APOCALYPSE . . . GOD'S WRATH . . . ANGRY WITNESSES . . . AWAKE!

Florian flung their prose down the lift shaft. The threatening literature fluttered between floors.

'And if you ever come back,' he yelled, using his hands as a megaphone, 'I'll bugger the pair of you!'

Florence was sleeping like a baby, a wisp of hair over one eye. Hands limply oustretched. Arms akimbo. Her armpits were shaven, but he forgave her that. She still had so much to learn!

He lay down gently beside her and discreetly sniffed at her. The animal aroma of the post-orgasmic female mingled with the scent of L'Heure Bleue. He kissed the curve of her shoulders and her lips. She awoke.

'My God,' she murmured, 'I fell asleep . . . What's the time? I must be getting back!'

She rose and began picking up her clothes. Suddenly she froze in astonishment. Her eyes widened and her mouth fell open soundlessly.

'What's the matter?' asked Nazulis.

'Florian, it's amazing!' she cried.

She was holding her head in both hands and uttering a sort of sob or laugh which she evidently could no longer contain.

'What is it then?' he said worriedly.

'Florian, Florian!' she stammered.

'Darling, tell me what is the matter?'

She bent her head and her eyes filled with tears. 'It's quite extraordinary,' she said, unable to believe the undeniable evidence. She walked around the room, naked, radiant – and upright. She no longer had a limp. 'It doesn't hurt any more! I can't feel the pain in my hip! Unbelievable! Miraculous!'

He went over to her and kissed her ear, beneath the tiny ringlets scented with L'Heure Bleue.

'It's no miracle,' he said calmly, 'it's just love, that's all. The only real therapy. But that is something the doctors will never tell you.'

'But how could the pain vanish like this? So completely?'

She paced back and forth, crying quietly to

115

herself, walking with a triumphant relish.

'The body is a single entity, all of a piece from head to toe, thyroid to anklebone, from intestines to imagination. Paul Valéry used to say: "The greatest poet is the nervous system".'

Florence continued to flex her legs and muscles. She was ecstatic.

'The body can be overwhelmingly content, to the very peak of its powers,' Florian went on. 'It opposes psychic or somatic disorders with all its strength. If it doesn't get its fair share of sexual pleasure (the intensest human fulfilment), the body just starts falling apart. So does the mind. There then follow all kinds of problems: the individual punishes him or herself with illness, as psychiatrists point out. Lack of sexual pleasure, or not enough of it, leads to serious disease, ill-health of one kind or another. Abstinence makes you ill. And chastity – whatever the priests and moralists say – is not a virtue but a sickness.'

'How does that apply to my hip trouble?' Florence asked him.

'Your desires ran into a brick wall. Your body had to confront the ban placed on its deepest desire. And in one sense it rebelled.'

She was examining her hip as if it were possible to perceive some cog which had been jamming the mechanism.

'Your body, for very complex reasons it might

116

be a wise idea to analyse, chose a precise spot at which to show its resentment: your hip. From the exact time your organism rediscovered its satisfaction, the rebellion ended and the pain disappeared.'

'It's extraordinary!' she exclaimed.

'It's normal,' he added. 'The only real antidote to illness is the complete satisfaction of one's desires.'

'I get the impression that I've just made love for the very first time,' Florence announced.

She was blooming, voluptuously thrusting out her arms in a huge stretch. Her small, youthful breasts jutted pertly. Florian admired her figure once again, finding his desire for her renewed.

'My husband doesn't think I'm sensual,' she said, abstractedly running a finger over a slight scratch on her shin. 'He thinks "all that sort of thing" doesn't interest me. We make love hurriedly, without saying a word, and then goodnight, that's it!'

Florian was intently stroking her buttocks. She was purring like a cat.

'As for myself,' he said, 'I have a friend called Agnes. We're not all that close, one might say. She thinks I'm impotent. With her I just can't get a hard on. It's not that she's unattractive, but there's simply something about her that – in my case, anyhow – inhibits or prevents erection. We've tried to make love on several occasions, but every time it ended in failure. She likes me a lot, she feels a sort of tender compassion for me, thinking I'm impotent with all women. It's never occurred to her that desire is selective.'

'My husband has such little interest in me,' Florence went on, 'and does it so perfunctorily that after . . . sex, I have to satisfy myself, on my own.'

'Is it then that you fantasise?' Florian asked her. He was sucking her nipples alternately. They hardened under his tongue.

'All those images which run through my head,' she said dreamily, 'when I give myself pleasure.'

'Tell me about them,' he said, excited now.

'Until today I used to think it was wrong. Forbidden images which had to be dispelled. So I'd go along to confession. I never felt at ease.'

'And you limped.'

'Yes. Inside myself I felt that something was not quite right. Now I know what I was missing. You've suddenly shown me my true self. I have an urgent need to be loved. I'm a sensual person.'

'Tell me your fantasies,' he said, dallying with her pubic curls. 'Describe what's showing in your erotic cinema.'

'First of all, that long, rigid, solid cock pointing at me . . . How often I dreamed of that! There's also a male torso, a muscular suntanned body which goes with it and comes to take me in its arms . . .'

Her eyes stared up at the ceiling, as if gazing at distant yet distinct pictures.

'Is that all?'

He had introduced the three middle fingers of his left hand into Florence's moist vagina and was moving them in a slow circular motion.

'I'm looking for your G-spot,' he said.

'With me,' she laughed, 'it's everywhere . . . Oh yes, go on like that . . . Oh that's good, that's good . . .'

Gulliver had sprung up hard as a poker. Florian positioned himself over Florence so that they could enjoy a variety of delightful pubic tickling and rub against one another.

'You brought me bliss with your mouth,' he said. 'Now I'd like to come deep inside you.'

'Oh yes!' she said.

She spread her legs and lay ready for him.

'I'm right with you,' she whispered as he gently sank into her.

They remained a while motionless, savouring the exquisite experience of penetration. A beatific Gulliver felt its sensitive head held by Florence's pulsing clonic clutch. From time to time she would contract her muscles, nipping and gripping the firm, rounded tip.

'Oh that's great, I love it, it's marvellous,' Florian blurted out, thinking that yes, all was well with him . . .

'Move inside me,' she urged.

He worked Gulliver's piston to and fro, deliberately, driving to its full length.

'Oh,' she said, 'I think I'm going to . . .'

'Wait for me,' he asked her. 'I'd rather we came together.'

They set up a gradual, perfectly synchronised rhythm. Florian's thrusts probed Florence's depths. Belly to belly, breast to breast, mouth glued to mouth, they went at it, driven by a force greater than themselves yet emanating from themselves. This was the moment, Florian knew, when the body simply took over. He was no longer in control of his – simply content to follow its intense journey. 'The finest stroll any human being ever takes', he told himself.

He let go completely.

The lower half of his body seemed to move of its own volition, pleasing itself, finding its own cadence, and Gulliver's head was swollen, its shaft dilated. Florian's heart doubled its beat. The blood seemed to congest yet throb powerfully below Florian's skin. All this strength sprang from some mysterious logic and all this instinctual energy converged to hasten the overwhelming seesaw into climax.

Florian felt himself surge forward, on the brink of overflow.

'I'm about . . .' he gasped.

'Yes, yes . . .'

'Together?'

'Yes . . . me too . . . with you,' she stammered.

Borne on their frenzied dance, they clung to each other wildly, bodies soldered together.

He clutched her hand as if she were on a death bed and about to take the final journey. Then the Great Earthquake seized them, hurling them onto the bed's furthest reaches before flinging them ashore once more, inert and stunned, their tongues tasting salt and in their ears that elusive shell-diffused sound of the sea.

6

ANGELS AND DEMONS

Florian's bag of equipment was ready. Transmitters, miniaturized aerials, batteries and all he required to install sensitive listening devices inside the four confessional boxes. Four systems fitted with the most sophisticated electronic gadgetry would allow Nazulis to gather at source everything our moral guides call 'sin' — uneasy whispers, stammered outpourings, furtively embarrassed admissions included.

This all-pervading notion of sin perturbed our oenologist considerably. The way most individuals would accuse themselves at the drop of a hat, solemnly prepared to repent of trifling or even imaginary offences, and assume what psychiatrists term culpability, both baffled and worried Nazulis.

He himself had escaped from this guilt syndrome donkeys' years ago. He'd come a long way since then. Now he would have to try hard to understand the subtle mechanisms of constant self-blame. How could intelligent twentieth century people still behave in this way? What thoughts went through their heads? How did this creeping sense of guilt spread to choke their pleasures and desires?

In order to find out, he had to listen to them. To listen to them he needed hidden mikes, and to place these he had to get himself locked inside the church overnight. Then no one could disturb his bugging activities . . .

His bag also contained assorted sandwiches, two bottles of Châteauneuf du Pape, one of Vieille Prune, and various other treats – to keep up his spirits during the night.

He arrived just before the doors of St Honoro were shut, at eight p.m. Hidden behind a pillar he waited until the verger turned off the lights one by one. Transept, roof, main altar, chapels, side rows, the saints in their niches – all entered the dark in turn. The ecclesiastical factotum took a last look round. Had he forgotten anything? He scratched one ear, then his arse, then aligned a chair that was not quite straight. It squeaked on the flagstones.

At last he pulled the heavy door behind him. Inside the deserted church now plunged into darkness the sound of the huge key double-locking the door was resoundingly audible.

Florian was alone.

For a long time he did not move. He was thinking of Florence, seeing once again her lovely face transformed by ecstasy, feeling her body blaze in successive orgasms.

All around him the thick, black night was unbroken save for one tiny luminous dot in the distance: it was the small red lamp burning above the shrine. When he was a child they'd assured him that while that red lamp shone it meant that Jesus was there.

'What if someone switched it off?' he'd asked the old woman who was coaching him in the Catechism. 'Does Jesus go away?'

'The lamp is always burning,' she replied sternly.

'What if there's a power cut?'

'Florian, when will you stop asking silly questions?'

'But if the lamp . . .'

'Be quiet. I don't want to hear your voice any more.'

The Catechism, he told himself, was like the Army: you didn't question it. You had to march, obey orders and shut your trap.

He laid his bag against a pillar and opened a bottle of 1970 Châteauneuf – a great year for Côtes du Rhône. The cork made a satisfying *plop* which seemed to echo through the entire building.

This was a wine high in alcohol content, probably even 15%, made from grapes ripened by the scorching sunshine of the Midi. Hardly giving his nose a chance, Florian gulped it down – almost the whole glassful, which was scarcely the wine buff's way. He was thirsty and needed sustenance.

He quaffed a second glass and a third in quick succession. It was a rich, fullbodied wine, but how it hit home! The church all at once seemed warm to Florian. He flashed his torch here and there. St Christopher, holding his staff and with a lamb swathed round his shoulders, was smiling at him.

He gnawed at a sandwich but he wasn't really hungry. He was still thirsty.

The Clos Saint-Jean was truly superb. He polished off the first bottle and opened the second, whose cork again resounded if anything even more welcomingly.

The deep red wine swilled down his gullet. He was enjoying its bouquet, its redolence of vines ripened in the furnace of Provence. He got up unsteadily and shone his torch again.

'The Church has its good points,' he muttered to himself euphorically, illuminating each niche with its saint. The statues held out their stone arms in friendly fashion and seemed to be smiling at Florian.

'What did I actually come here to do?' he wondered.

He could not remember. Meanwhile, now for the Vieille Prune. Excellent. Another glass. Better still: this was a most fortifying and inspiriting beverage indeed.

Suddenly his head slumped. Florian fell over, and into a deep sleep.

There was a shout which filled the whole church.

'Come and see, come and see!' St Christopher was yelling. The saint was floating twenty feet above the ground.

'How do you manage to fly?' asked Florian.

'I put down my staff and my lamb and flap my wings like the angels. Quite simple. All you need do is move your wings to and fro!'

Florian raised his wings and took off without difficulty.

'Good heavens!' he cried. 'I'm flying!'

The two men swooped from one corner of the church to the other.

'Shall we take a trip?' Florian suggested.

'If you like.'

They opened a window and ascended into the starry night. The Place Victor Hugo dwindled in the distance and was soon no more than a luminous dot among all the others on the earth.

The two celestial cosmonauts soared like birds

through the firmament.

'I'd like very much to meet the female angels,' Florian said.

'Don't you know that angels have no sex?'

'Not even a little one? Not even the merest vestige of a working one?'

'No. Nothing. There's just a smooth expanse.'

'But then how do they – ?'

'They don't,' said St Christopher. 'They play music.'

'Music. What music?'

'In front of God they sing Bach. Among themselves, Mozart.'

'What about Schubert?' asked Florian.

'They play Schubert when they're sad.'

'Are we going to see God?' Florian inquired.

'God?' said St Christopher. 'What God? What God? What God?'

His voice faded. Suddenly, with a wingbeat, he vanished.

Nazulis woke with a start. He looked at his watch. It was seven a.m.

Someone had opened the church doors. Footsteps could be heard.

He hastily gathered up his things and concealed himself behind a pillar. A group of nuns were heading towards him. They passed very close, their coifs like great white birds astride their heads. The last in line, slightly behind the

128

others, filed by Nazulis, so near him that he felt a waft of air from her hat as she scurried past.

She caught sight of him.

They looked at each other for a second, eyes wide in mutual amazement. She was very young, a novice of no more than twenty. Despite the severity of her habit, she could not altogether disguise her natural beauty. Nuns as beautiful as that, thought the astonished Florian, were only usually seen in the movies . . . The whites of her eyes reminded him of porcelain, the pupils a bright cornflower blue. Her full red lips contrasted with the pallor of her skin. Her mouth amazingly resembled that of Monica Vitti. It was not the odour of sanctity she exuded but an extremely alluring fleshly charm.

'Sssh . . .!' said Florian, his finger to his lips.

There was in this young beauty's glance something dazzling. Her sisters' procession had now moved considerably further on. Florian had a sudden irrational urge. He lowered his head and lunged forward under the starched bonnet, a wing of which brushed his forehead lightly. And he kissed the young woman full on the lips.

She was so stunned that she stayed where she was, incapable of any reaction. The kiss lasted a second – an eternity. Did she recall Baudelaire's phrase: *A minute's bliss for an eternity's damnation?* Of course not! Baudelaire isn't read in convents.

While the clock was about to register a second second, the nun's lips trembled and left Florian's. He had had time (for his hunter's instincts were acute), to run a hand over this angelic Eve's breasts and to feel how they had been flattened by some tight nunnish cummerbund or probationary bandage. What a waste! he thought.

She fled and left the young man walking on air, in a sort of mystic levitation, upon his tranced lips the taste of wonder. At least just once in her life – Florian mused, on coming down to earth again – she'd have had a fleeting glimpse of human experience to give her something to conjure with, during those long lonely nights.

Nazulis returned home jubilant. He took a shower and shaved to the strains of his beloved Schubert's *German dances*.

'Life is great!' he murmured, dabbing two drops of Acqua di Selva behind each ear. The scent of pine wafted to his nostrils. He went over and replaced the record in its sleeve. Then he pressed the *Messages* button on his answering machine.

'So what's up?' a female voice cut in. 'Are you out of circulation or something? Ring me back then. Here's a big kiss.'

'Who's she?' Florian wondered, racking his brains. But he could not place her and meanwhile the next message was delivered in loud, well-spoken masculine tones.

'Hello, brother dear. I'm off tomorrow for Acongagua. Look after Mother, she tends to worry about me. We'll see each other in two months. Cheers!'

Florian's brother was a mountaineering freak. He had taken part in the first French expedition to conquer Everest, led by Giscard's former minister, Pierre Mazeaud. Whenever the opportunity arose, he would go off to the Himalayas or wherever else there were new summits to be climbed. Whenever he left for these remote mountains (and Florian himself would go to the ends of the earth to meet Javanese, Guinean, Brazilian or any other exotic examples of femininity), their mother would arrange on one mantelpiece photographs, locks of hair, items of clothing and so on. This sort of primitive shrine was to protect the traveller throughout his expedition, and so far the ritual had always worked.

After a new tone beep on the tape, he heard a familiar voice.

'Darling hello, it's me, Ariane. The Lambertinis are throwing a big party tomorrow evening. I'd love you to take me along as I don't like going to

131

their kind of do all on my own. So call me back, lover!'

The message had been recorded the previous evening, which meant the party was that evening. Florian dialled Ariane's number.

'Hello, it's me,' he said.

'Delighted you called, poppet. Are you coming to the Lambertini's party? All the best orgiasts in Paris will be there – movie people, singers, media celebrities . . . Toledo's going . . . .'

'Sabrina too?' asked Nazulis.

'Sabrina Ducelli? Oh yes, and Poppy, Mado, Ricou, the River-Berthoux couple . . . All the trendy partygoers . . .'

'I couldn't give a shit about the River-Berthouxes. I'll come along as soon as Sabrina arrives.'

'But you will look after me just a little, won't you poppet? Mmm?'

'Mmm.'

'I'll call by to pick you up tonight at ten . . . Ah, I almost forgot – the theme of the party is Animals. Fancy dress disguise, masks, the choice is yours. I'm going as Mickey Mouse.'

'I don't like fancy dress,' said Florian.

'Just this once,' she pleaded, 'do make a bit of an effort.'

He pondered for a moment. 'I'll come as an elephant,' he said.

132

It was an imposing Avenue Foch flat, only a stone's throw from the Etoile, and with its own immaculate garden. The three or four prostitutes whose particular beat covered the hundred yards or so of pavement opposite, watched incredulously as a veritable Noah's Ark of brilliant creatures began to arrive at the Lambertinis'.

Beasts of the jungle, lions, panthers, tigers, assorted birds, ostriches with flower-decorated rumps, big furry bears, several apes — masks gaping in grotesque surprise – and even a little plump chap wearing a pink piggy mask.

Hugo Lambertini, the famous Italian millionaire and Europe's clothes-chain king, had one of the finest apartments in Paris. There he liked to throw parties which were in turn sumptuous, riotous and orgiastic. He would invite the capital's most debauched set – the best-looking women, the most perverted girls, the craziest men and the smartest caterers.

A raucous and joyful din filled the main reception room: friendly greetings, mutual compliments on costumes, popping of champagne corks, squeals of women being groped, laughter and loud conversation . . . Things were warming up.

In a corner musicians in white satin uniforms were playing jazz: a quartet comprised of tenor sax, piano, bass and drums.

133

The hosts welcomed Ariane and Florian with their native Italian exuberance. Hugo was wearing a splendid mask of a horse's head with a mane of silky white hair which trailed over his shoulders. He doffed his mask to greet his guests, kissed Ariane's hand and shook Florian's, then resumed his equine metamorphosis.

'How nice to see you?' he exclaimed volubly. 'Ariane or should I say Mickey, you're always so beautiful . . . Do you know my wife Giulietta?'

Giulietta had contrived an amazing head-dress of multi-coloured feathers which turned her into an exotic macaw.

Florian kissed the bird's hand. With a connoisseur's glance he appraised the creature's shape –which was in no sense disguised. An attractive, well-preserved body, recently tanned by a sun-lamp or a tropical trip. Giulietta certainly knew how to move that figure of hers to best advantage – and she had a roving eye.

'Make yourselves at home. Eat, drink and be merry,' the Italian stallion urged them excitedly.

Then he left (*Scusi, scusi*) to greet a doe accompanied by a deer with an impressive spread of antlers. The pair seemed to have just emerged from a thicket: they had the uneasy, startled look of forest animals listening for human footsteps.

'Pity you're not in fancy dress,' said Ariane as Florian led her towards an opulent buffet heaped with gastronomic delights.

'Not in fancy dress?' he said, delving into a plate of caviare. 'You'll see, soon enough.'

They went for a walk in the garden, where there was another buffet table. Florian quaffed another glass of Dom Pérignon and helped himself to another Beluga canapé. Yes, he thought, feeling the tiny eggs dissolve against his teeth, life was treating him well.

They sauntered through the vast apartment's many rooms. Half naked creatures pursued each other down the corridors, giggling. Under their disguises the women shrieked and squealed, stirring up the surrounding jungle. They jostled, goosed each other, embraced and kissed.

In one room illumined by a pale blue light a Mickey Mouse ('Another!' exclaimed the irritated Ariane) lay on the floor, dress hitched up, being fucked by the little pink piggy-man. The latter was out of breath and straining to satisfy his partner, who wore big black ears which joggled in time with his buttocks. He was failing, however.

'Go and try someone else!' the other Mickey, irate and frustrated, screamed at him.

He pulled up the laughing hog's mask which then stayed perched on his head. Like that he presented a strange, doubly porcine picture: the false – grinning and pink, and the real – miserable and pink.

In another room, beneath a seven-branched candelabra frolicked a calmly copulating couple.

On all fours on the white moquette, the woman had thrust out her splendid, chubby buttocks. She was virtually naked, wearing only a flimsy panther skin, and Florian felt sure he had seen that arse somewhere before. It was being offered to the thrusting prick of a very hirsute man kneeling behind her. Over his head was a bull's muzzle, whose glass eyes shone with an odd yellow glow. It was an extraordinary spectacle, bull covering panther, the thrusts slow and regular.

Her weight on the palms of her hands, legs splayed, the woman let herself be fucked in silence. The fourteen flames of the two chandeliers flickered. From the sitting-room filtered the sound of the quartet, starting in on a Thelonious Monk number. The man's breath sounded wheezy beneath his taurine headgear.

'Florian, it's you!' the panther exclaimed.

'Sabrina, darling!' he cried.

He leaned down to peck the fair Sabrina on both cheeks, while she maintained her position – glued to the minotaur. The latter had not yet finished and was plunging to and fro with metronomic regularity.

'Oh, I'm really glad to see you!' Sabrina said.

Florian made the introductions, ignoring the

bovine fucker, who went gasping on.

'Ariane, this is the divine Sabrina! But maybe you already know each other?'

'Not really,' Ariane said with a thin little smile.

She instinctively held out her hand and at once recognised the absurdity of the gesture. To regain her composure she adjusted her round mouse-ears, tugging at each in turn.

'How's your work going these days?' Sabrina enquired. 'Your arse-essay, your wines, and those articles . . .?'

'Everything all right with you?' Florian said.

The horned beast continued thrusting, quite excluded from the conversation.

'Is Poppy here?' asked Sabrina, her bottom aloft and still being poked to a steady beat: one stroke, two strokes, pause; one stroke, two strokes, pause; one stroke, two . . .

'I haven't seen her yet,' Nazulis said. 'How about you, did you come with your husband?'

'He's over there,' the panther indicated with a nod of her head. 'Right now he's being absolutely awful to me, really horrid . . .'

'That's marriage for you,' said Florian authoritatively.

There was a silence. The candles flickered. Piano and bass were now embarking on an old Louis Armstrong tune. A waiter with a tray passed round glasses of champagne.

'Can you put a glass on the side for me?' Sabrina requested, turning her head towards Florian. 'For the time being I'm . . . busy.'

The metronomic bull suddenly stopped pounding away and snapped his fingers for the waiter. Then he took the bull mask by the horns and ripped it off his head, emitting yet another sigh.

'What a wanker!' exclaimed Florian. 'That's Jean-Pierre Soudard, the Channel One presenter,' he whispered in Ariane's ear.

Still on his knees, still plugging that pert pink posterior, Soudard did not deign (or did not dare) turn towards Nazulis and Ariane. Looking haggard and dishevelled he stared glassily in front of him, with something of MacEnroe's determinedly vacant expression during a change-over.

Soudard seized a glass from the tray offered, knocked back his drink and replaced it. Then he pulled on the massive head again. He had not once looked at Sabrina's friends. He needs to hide his identity, Florian thought: has to preserve his image!

Protected by his mask the bull resumed his relentless motion, his hands gripping the beauteous panther's hips. In – out, pause. In – out, pause . . . He had a sturdy, medium-sized pizzle protruding from a black thicket from which swung the bollocks, one large, the other somewhat smaller.

138

'He's better than on telly,' Florian whispered in Sabrina's ear.

She chuckled, still propped on her forearms.

'I mean,' Florian went on, 'that here he's a bit more forceful.'

Soudard was the most deadpan newscaster (and the most quickfire, come to that) on any current affairs programme on French TV. His huge hairy hands would rest on the news-desk, on either side of the microphone, and with his staring eyes riveted to the autocue, he would talk down to the whole of France every weekend. As he droned on, reducing every item to a self-important newscast monotone, Soudard seemed to embody that relentlessly false impartiality endemic to the tube.

Horns lowered, the taurine personality ploughed on, obsessed with his incessant grinding to and fro.

Florian winked at Sabrina.

'Here at least,' he concluded, 'he keeps his mouth shut.'

Nazulis was thirsty. He headed for the buffet once more. Ariane followed suit, never letting him out of her sight.

'Don't you want to . . . cut loose and enjoy

yourself a bit?' he asked her.

'How about you?' she inquired. 'Do you?'

'Right now I've got quite a thirst. I'll show you my fancy dress after we've had some champagne.'

They passed through the flat again. The atmosphere of sexual heat was rapidly being fanned into flame.

An orang-utang lying on his back in the middle of a corridor was having his organ oralized by a slimly built antelope, whose lyre-shaped horns bobbed about as the caress progressed. Meanwhile this same ape ate, through his mask, an attractive blonde who squatted over him. She herself wore only a black mask which concealed the top half of her face. Crouching over the simian snout, she had adopted the normal posture of female urination, but at that particular moment she seemed to be deriving considerably greater pleasure. Then the animals changed places, the blonde on the doe and the ape upon the blonde.

'Delightful!' Florian enthused.

Further on, inside the large room which adjoined the sitting room, the carnival of the animals was in full swing. A score of couples were entwined in all sorts of positions and groups, kissing, sniffing, sucking and fucking, then taking turn and turn about in a constant sexual exchange. Nearly all of them had removed their

140

masks and fancy dress.

Florian recognized a Minister, another television personality, a well-known comedian and an eminent media doctor who looked like a cowboy. The jungle was flailing about in a state of extreme agitation. Rustles, bestial noises, gasps, sobs, slitherings, lapping sounds, sometimes a brief grunt, but never a word spoken.

The oenologist's nostrils quivered; his nose wrinkled in distaste. Florian pulled a face: male odours, more than anything, tended to put him off. He stayed cool, however, resolving to ignore these animal aromas.

He needed to get in the mood. He went off to find a bottle of champagne which he had concealed in an ingle nook. After drinking three glasses in quick succession, he undressed.

'Look at my outfit,' he said to Ariane.

He dropped his trousers. Ariane's jaw dropped with them. She stared in stupefaction.

'But . . . but . . .' she managed to splutter.

CARNIVAL OF THE ANIMALS

'Not bad, is it?' Florian said.

'But . . . It looks incredibly realistic!' she exclaimed.

'Yes, doesn't it. A whopper of a chopper.'

'Where did you . . .?'

'It's from Hong Kong. Present from a friend. I've never tried it on before but I think it suits me, don't you?'

'As fancy dress it's a bit excessive, I'd say,' the young woman reflected.

'Moulded in special plastic and covered in some very supple organic material . . . Feel!'

She could not bring herself to do so. It was too enormous. Finally he put it in her hand.

'You'd think it was the genuine article,' she said in amazement. 'The texture, colour, even the pink tip . . .'

'Only this one is knee-length! That's the main difference!'

After several more glasses of Dom Pérignon, he strolled around the couples to see what effect his elephantine appendage would have upon them. He sauntered about, stark naked and quite at ease, swaggering exaggeratedly.

As he passed, couples stopped to peer and stare at him, often even pulling apart in order to do so. The guests nudged each other, incredulous.

Silence fell upon the room.

Florian cleared his throat as if to make a speech. All eyes were fixed upon him. Only one middle-aged man continued screwing, well into the alluring charms of a redhead nymphet who looked distinctly under-age. After a moment even this absorbed satyr realised that everything had gone strangely silent. He turned his head and saw in astonishment Nazulis, virtually standing over him, staring scornfully at him, to boot. The arrogant pendant quivered threateningly like a truncheon.

At that the grizzled orgiast grabbed his Lolita and dragged her out of the room, both in considerable disarray. I must have triggered off his complexes, thought Florian – amazed by such a reaction.

His trunk dangling between his legs he went off to refill his champagne glass. He staggered slightly but kept his head, and his tail too, as it were, for the latter had been slipped over, and firmly affixed to, the luckless Gulliver's head.

The pendulous device had a devastating effect.

Word went round that 'there was a man who . . . a stud with a . . . yes, as big as your arm . . . phenomenal!' People drifted in to see for themselves, and all eyes were mesmerised by what they saw.

Nazulis was rather pleased to be the cynosure. He looked regally around him. A crowd had gathered to view the prodigy. The men were especially miffed, becoming almost physically ill at the sight. Wracked by shame, they tried hiding their more modest dongs behind their hands, making nests of their nervous fingers so as to protect their own sensitive fledglings.

The women, by contrast, were wide-eyed and almost drooled. Incredulity and/or lust were clearly evident.

The silence had become suffocating. The musicians too had been informed of the miracle and they also were craning for a glimpse. You could hear the proverbial pin drop.

Nazulis climbed onto a chair and raised his chin in a Mussolinian motion. The crowd had formed a circle, respectfully keeping its distance.

'He's going to say something!' someone whispered.

The Elephant-Dick-Man cleared his throat and

began his speech.

'Ladies and Gentlemen, a brief word only, because I don't want to interrupt your pleasurable activities. Your silence and surprise, surprise *me*. It seems my splendid appendage arouses in you some very strong, confused and secret emotions. All small boys have friendly cock-contests, the largest winning most respect. Do you think the same applies to adults?

'Everyone's fascinated with the phallic. Regal sceptres, military swagger-sticks and cannons, menhirs, obelisks, and missiles of every variety . . . Who has the finest war-head?

'What, ladies and gentleman, does this general veneration for the masculine projectile or projection and its symbolism *mean*?

'I crave your attention now because we have reached the very nub of the problem. I see here some analysts and medical men. I doubt if they'd contradict what I'm saying . . . The rogue you see between my legs hypnotises you because it is the symbol of human power.

'And here's the rub. This is the mistake everybody makes: THE SYMBOLIC IS NOT THE REAL. Gigantic pricks do not necessarily imply enormous power. Sometimes extremely potent men are equipped with quite modest weapons. As that great writer Colette, who knew a thing or two about men, remarked: 'Better a lively little one than a dozy big one.' Napoleon, that notorious fucker, had a bauble of barely ten centimetres, a child's willie. By comparison, you see village idiots, abulic thickos and impotent morons trailing things thrice as long around with them.

'Look at all those bodybuilders with bulging muscles, pumping iron. Are they really so strong? Take any contest or sport you like, they're no match for any opponent with so-called 'normal' muscles. They're puffed up windbags, full of bluff.

'So, ladies and gentlemen, this mighty weapon I've enjoyed showing off tonight – since it is, after all, an animal fancy dress party – this engine you find so fascinating, this too is all a bluff. Look!'

Nazulis twisted a valve and tapped at the tube. There was a slight suction noise and the audience suddenly gasped as if in relief.

Gulliver, tried and tested, normal Gulliver reappeared. The show was over.

Murmurs of satisfaction could be heard now, and the room's occupants returned to their previous pursuits. Couples, trios and foursomes re-formed. The jazz quartet once more took up their instruments. The champagne corks popped as frequently as before. The wind of panic had blown over.

'You ought to be in politics. You speak well,'

Sabrina said, resplendently naked under her fur.

Florian replaced the chair which had been his soap box.

'Certainly not,' he replied. 'I value my soul too much. Come on, let's have a drink.'

Ariane followed them despite her wretched Mickey Mouse rig, which seemed glued to her head; its huge ears never remained in place but would keep flopping over, first one then the other. They all found the buffet in the garden deserted. The night air was cool and Sabrina pressed shivering against Florian, who was still stark naked.

'Come on,' she said. 'Let's get warm.'

With Ariane-Mickey dogging their footsteps, they found a cosy corner back inside the apartment – an empty bed. Sleeping or embracing couples lay on the floors, scattered here, there and everywhere. Nearly all of them had shed their masks and fancy dress outfits. They caught a glimpse of the bull-headed Soudard who was shafting the lady of the house in the main sitting room, with his usual rhythmic verve, as if powered by a diesel engine.

'What stamina!' Sabrina marvelled.

'Is he good at it?' Mickey asked.

'Very mechanical.'

'Anyhow he's setting some kind of record,' Florian observed. 'He's preserving his anonymity to the bitter end. I'm amazed he hasn't suffocated himself yet.'

Someone else, too, had kept on his mask, doubtless believing he might be marginally more seductive thus: little Mr Piggy. With his leering porker's snout he was wandering from room to room, looking for love. But his small, paunchy and wrinkled body was finding no takers.

'Poor little chap!' Mickey murmured.

'He should have disguised himself from head to foot,' said Florian. 'He'd have had better luck that way.'

Just then the pig approached them.

'Great party, hee hee!' he squealed in his high-pitched voice, appropriately porcine even through his mask.

He began unceremoniously pinching Sabrina's and Ariane's breasts.

'Shall *we* party? Shall we, then?'

Panther, Mickey and Florian rapidly escaped into the depths of the apartment.

Strewn all over the carpets were what might be called animal-droppings – disguises, masks, feathers, costume, bras, panties, false wings and other colourful litter – while their owners drowsed, snored or flailed and twitched in the last spasms of lust.

A naked girl passed. Her hair was dishevelled and she was vacantly smoking a joint. She picked

149

her way through the recumbent bodies, as if heading for some somnambulists' convention. They noticed a red paper rose projecting from the cleft in her buttocks as she glided along. Was she socialist or poet? Nazulis wondered. At any rate she was keeping a cheekily tight arse to the world, come who might.

The two women and Florian finally found an unoccupied room whose big bed had an enticing multi-coloured coverlet. They lay down, with Sabrina on Florian's right, Ariane on his left.

Gulliver reared its head on scenting Sabrina. Her skin smelt fresh and natural, and exuded an undefinable scent of ozone. Florian had never encountered such an unusual, alluring aroma; it had intrigued and excited him when they had first met. He had never had enough time to appreciate it however.

She stretched luxuriously, writhing sensuously while Florian stroked and sniffed her in delight. He undid the strings holding up her panther skin and took it off. Ariane meanwhile doffed her Mickey Mouse mask and shook out her long dark hair which released its cloud of sleek scents (Lancome's *Magie Noire*). The olfactory organ of Florian was fully occupied with Sabrina though; he himself was leaning over her inhaling in silent admiration. She had a superb, slim blonde body, sleekly muscled as much as conventionally curvaceous. The silken tufts under her armpits had been artfully tended: they were neither too bushy nor too long. How fine she smelt! Gulliver reared in ecstatic fervour, ready for a treat.

Nimbly ducking, Florian tickled Sabrina's stomach with his hair and then his face descended further still, towards that blonde promontory of hers. He was just about to open her when he remembered Soudard – in a sudden vision of that yellow-eyed bull's mask, and that pizzle working its way in and out, to and fro. The small screen filled by that inane smile . . . Those bollocks, the big and the small, swinging about in their pouch to that remorseless pendulum rhythm.

All things considered, he settled for Sabrina's upper lips, kissing these fervently and leaving Gulliver to find its own way through the lower depths.

'Who's kissed you tonight?' Florian asked her.

'On the mouth?' said Sabrina. 'Nobody. I've been fucked by three or four animals that's all. I haven't had a single kiss.'

'Good,' said Florian.

He kissed her in leisurely style. Her mouth tasted of fruit. Meanwhile Ariane, not wanting to be left out, had moved her head downwards: she began licking the drowsy dormouse with little flicks of her tongue. Since she scarcely ever watched television she was not afflicted with

151

Soudardic allergy. Her tongue dabbled amid the golden thatch, prompting groans of pleasure from Sabrina. These reverberated inside Florian's mouth.

Gulliver, still wandering across the blonde scrubland, encountered Ariane's mouth. The young woman's lips left the wet cleft a moment to clamp upon the tense lance whose tip quivered with impatience. Ariane's tongue then worked on the creature's pink bulb, which became harder and redder every second. Florian and Sabrina continued kissing, occasionally pausing to murmur mutual terms of endearment.

'I want you,' he was whispering.

'And I want you too,' she sighed.

'You're lovely, so beautiful. You're an angel. You . . .'

She crushed her mouth against Florian's greedily, devouring it. Gulliver could no longer bear the strain. Somewhere, somehow, the explosion simply had to come. Ariane felt it coming. She accentuated her pressures, speeding up her movements. But Florian pulled away with a wriggle of his hips and plunged deep into the wet, wide-open Sabrina.

She uttered a cry, caught unawares by such an access of pleasure.

Gulliver, like a diver, was moving with long, leisurely strokes through the strange, silent world beneath the delta. Pushed and pulled by Florian, the beast let go, rocked upon the surf which was bearing them aloft.

Ariane, who definitely did not want to remain inactive herself, licked her forefinger and stuck it between Florian's buttocks.

'Hey, take it easy, go slow!' he urged.

He realised that with all this stimulus he could not hold back much longer.

'Sabrina, I'm going to come,' he said.

Ariane grabbed one of Florian's hands and thrust it upon her own pubic thatch, moving furiously up and down. Nazulis promptly worked his middle finger inside her vulva.

'I'm going to come!' Florian repeated desperately.

Sabrina clutched him tightly in her arms and jammed her loins as hard as she could against his.

'Me too,' she gasped.

'Me too,' Ariane interjected.

The three of them came almost simultaneously. But differently, of course. One of the women uttered a series of exclamations, the other emitted a kind of guttural sob, and Florian shuddered in a fiery spasm of pleasure but said not a word.

The actual experience of orgasm is invariably individual, never similar.

'Wake up!'

A hand was shaking the entwined and sleeping troilists: three tangled bodies, half a dozen arms, half a dozen legs, together linked.

'Come on, wake up,' Hugo Lambertini repeated. 'It's six a.m.!'

'What . . . what is it?' mumbled a dazed Florian, frowning himself awake.

'We're all off to have breakfast at R.'s place. Get dressed, everyone's waiting for you.'

R. was a young Secretary of State who was both dynamic and ambitious, a politician who knew which way the wind was blowing and how to bide his time. He lived in a luxury flat near the Bastille. He too had quite a reputation as a partygiver. He had invited all those who had stayed over at his friend Hugo's.

'We're all going to go by Métro!' Lambertini declared.

'By Métro?' Florian said in amazement, rubbing his eyes.

'Yes. A nice democratic gesture, eh? The last time I took the Métro was . . . was . . .'

The millionaire furrowed his brow, delving in the mists of memory.

'Prior to 1981, it must have been. Yes, that's it, it was October 1980 . . . A really fascinating experience . . .'

'Let's get going, come on!' various guests were

154

urging. They had shed their animal costumes and reverted to human clothing. Long evening dresses, crumpled dinner jackets, and in some cases jeans and plimsolls – the contents of wardrobes and drawers had certainly been ransacked.

The group – forty-five survivors of the previous evening's shenanigans – emerged into the cool morning air. At this hour the Avenue Foch was deserted. Only one elderly whore, her mouth a messy smear of paint, optimistically persevered along her beat. They greeted her with laughter and made for the Étoile, staggering, dancing, singing or fooling around.

From a distance they resembled those processions of bleary dawn revellers in Fellini films. The only thing missing was music by Nino Rota.

They funnelled onto the platform at Étoile-Charles de Gaulle just as the 6.33 train to Vincennes pulled in.

Assorted labourers and factory employees abroad watched the exclusive bunch of merry-makers pile into the leading coach.

'It's terrific!' Giulietta Lambertini was gushing, and she clapped her hands to display sparklers worth thousands of wage packets, glittering around fingers, wrists and neck. 'Absolutely ter-rific, the Métro. What a super idea!'

'Don't you think it's a bit rash showing off all these rocks to the plebs?' Hugo asked one of his friends, a man who owned a group of factories. 'They're insured, naturally, but . . .'

'Not to worry, old fellow,' the friend retorted. 'At 6 a.m. there are never any pickpockets, rapists or muggers on the Métro. What would they have to gain? Just take a look around you!'

The early morning cleaners and shift-workers, huddled in their seats, their eyes bloodshot from all the hours of sleep they'd missed out on, observed these interlopers impassively, indeed with no reaction whatever.

'It runs on rubber, these days, then!' Hugo reflected with some surprise. 'The last time I rode on the Métro it had iron wheels.'

'Well, these people deserve some creature comforts don't they, even if they are from North Africa.'

'Oh what fun!' Giulietta cried. 'I adore the Métro, it's quite an adventure. I find it exciting, as well.'

She teetered off down the compartment, star-ing at the workmen and immigrant labourers. She looked each of them up and down in fascination, inspecting them as if they were extra-terrestrials. This was a red-letter day for her.

'It gets me excited, really!' she exclaimed, rolling her eyes.

She went up to Soudard, who had retained his mask, no matter what. He was determined on anonymity at all costs. He alone among the delighted throng of chic ticket-holders stood erect, his hand tightly gripping the vertical bar in the standing area.

'Fuck me again!' she said to him, hoisting up her dress. Her naked buttocks were small and tanned.

'I – I can't!' protested the media-man, shaking his horns from side to side. 'I can't, not here.'

'I want you to,' she persisted.

The train entered the Concorde station. Two immigrant workers alighted quietly, their manner self-effacing, and they went on their way not glancing to right or left. Another got on board: this one had a small moustache, his face was gaunt and blue-jowled and his eyes looked forlorn. On seeing the fashionable crowd in the compartment – their finery, flashing jewels and bare legs, and those hands heavy with gold and precious stones waving champagne bottles – not to mention that character in a bull mask – the new passenger had just enough time to dash into the next carriage before the doors shut.

'Take me!' Giulietta urged as the train put on speed.

She had plastered herself against Soudard, her dress hitched high and her arse pressed into his flies, which she had wasted no time undoing.

'I can't . . .' he kept protesting.

'Yes you can! *Cretino!*' she screamed.

A few feet away from them, various black and white stalwarts of the labour-force contemplated the scene with stolid impassivity, far too tired to react.

'Are you going to do it?' Giulietta complained, wiggling her petite bottom feverishly against the horned man.

Nothing doing. A platonic halfwit.

'Please, Giulietta . . .' he was groaning under his mask, 'not now . . .'

'Imbecile, bullshitter, *filio de puta, ragazzo di niente, paparazzo di merda* . . .'

'I beg you . . .' Soudard duly begged.

They arrived at the Bastille stop. The in-crowd got out. Bullhead charged onto the platform gratefully. One of the revellers had a bright idea involving a bit of bravado.

'Proletarians, workers!' he yelled at the seated passengers.

Some of the latter slowly gazed through the glass at this troublemaker stirring it up.

'Workers, hey, drones!' he again shouted.

Then he very deliberately slapped his right bicep with his left palm. The clenched right fist

158

shot towards them in a sweepingly unmistakable obscene jerk. His friends on the platform fell about, slapping their thighs delightedly. Hugo was helpless with laughter.

The traindriver, who had kept the group in his sights since Étoile-Charles de Gaulle, braked abruptly and reversed. The incredulous Hugo and his companions saw the doors reopen.

'Now we're for it!' Nazulis murmured. Despite his better judgement he had gone along with this charade in bad taste – which now looked like misfiring.

'They're going to clobber us!' shouted Soudard, who was already sprinting for the exit.

The conductor had now stuck his head out of his window, waiting for the punch-up. But nothing happened. No one got out of the carriages. All the workers – immigrants, skivvies and wage-slaves – remained seated to a man, limply and correctly glued to their places, their eyes heavy with sleep. They hardly saw the carousers scattering down the corridors of the Bastille – and thereby hangs yet another symbol.

Florian would have liked to end the night (and start his day) with Sabrina, but it was impossible to shake off Ariane, who clung to him like a leech. So he accompanied them both to the trendy politician's door, where they were easily persuaded to continue partying.

He hailed a taxi.

'69 Rue des Saints-Pères,' he told the driver.

At this early hour Paris was not yet choked with traffic. Pigeons were swooping about. The taxi went along the Quais. Notre-Dame looked lovelier than ever, its stately architecture towering over flowering trees.

'Nice day,' said the driver.

Florian snorted assent. He didn't feel like talking. How beautiful the town looked after an orgy, he thought.

He climbed his stairs two by two, in a hurry to get into a bath. On the landing a man was waiting for Nazulis, revolver pointed at him.

'I'm Mireille's husband,' the man said.

8

A QUICK ONE – AND A TALE OF PARALLEL TRAINS

'Have you been waiting long?' Florian asked.

'Since last night.'

The man was tall and thin, with receding hair. He wasn't bad looking for all his menacing air and set jaw. The revolver he held was shaking a bit.

It was the first time Nazulis had had a firearm pointed expressly at himself. A long, gleaming tubular object that needed only a finger to crook and so beckon you rapidly to the next world. The man trained his weapon straight at Florian's chest. He seemed exhausted.

Florian was not afraid. He was not particularly courageous (he had a generalised fear of violence, madness and duplicity), but he did have self-confidence. He knew things usually went his way: life treated him pretty well on the whole.

He searched his pockets for the key. The man was still aiming his gun threateningly.

'Do come in,' said the oenologist. 'Would you

care for a coffee? I mean, you've been here since yesterday evening, isn't that so?'

'Since eleven p.m.,' said Mireille's husband.

'I'm sorry I kept you waiting so long. I expect you've come to talk to me about Mireille.'

'I've come to kill you.'

'Ah.'

Florian scratched his nose for a moment. Then he pinched his earlobe. He stared at the man somewhat curiously.

'Would you let me make you a coffee?' he asked him.

'I'll follow you in. No tricks, right? If you try anything, I'll shoot.'

Florian found a saucepan, emptied half a bottle of Evian into it and waited till the water boiled. He poured it over some fresh-ground Colombian coffee and picked out a couple of cups and some sugar. He poured out the coffee.

'Here, give me that,' he said, taking the revolver by its barrel.

The movement was so natural that the man did not resist. Florian put the shooter on the kitchen sideboard and passed a steaming cup to the man, who was shaking.

'Why did you want to kill me?'

'Because you're Mireille's lover.'

'Oh,' said Florian in a tone intended to stress the sheer anticlimactic unimportance of such a trifle. 'Among others . . . One of many, if I might say so . . Nothing in that to go over the top for.'

'I love my wife,' the husband definitively declared.

'Fine,' Florian agreed. 'I quite understand. She's a terrific woman. She's charming, attractive, she . . .'

'That's enough!' the man shouted, lurching forward to retrieve his gun.

He was too far from the sideboard to reach it in time. Florian had been too quick for him.

'Tut, tut,' he said, pocketing the revolver.

The weapon was surprisingly heavy. He realised why cops and robbers never keep their guns in their pockets: no trousers could withstand the strain of steel freight for long.

'I wonder if you haven't been reading too many bad thrillers,' Florian remarked. ' "Husband kills wife's lover". That sort of thing is fine for readers of *True Detective*. But we're no longer living in the nineteenth century. Morality is rather more relaxed these days. Women are liberated, thank God. One lover? Three? Why not? Mireille is a free agent, a consenting adult. She knows her mind . . . Anyway, how did you discover she was, so to speak, "deceiving" you?'

'I had my suspicions. I had her followed. A private investigator got me all the details and your address.'

Nazulis burst out laughing.

'This is just like a B-movie! A detective – with magnifying glass and binoculars!' He doubled up with mirth. 'A private eye who slides along walls, hides in bedrooms, sniffs the sheets and takes notes . . . Old chap, you're a romantic!'

'I love my wife,' the man repeated. 'You can't know how much I love her. I never get the urge to be unfaithful to her. I could never do without her. She's the only one . . .'

Florian found such amorous intensity affecting. He remained silent, lost in thought. From the flat below filtered some strains of ragtime. He recognized a Scott Joplin tune.

'And what about you?' the husband enquired. 'What is she to you? Do you love her?'

'She's a good and loyal friend,' Florian replied.

'But – do you love her?'

'Not like you,' he said.

He refilled their coffee cups.

'A love like yours,' Nazulis said, 'is admirable and very appropriate. I can't let myself intrude on it – not any longer. I won't see Mireille any more. I promise you that.'

The man gazed at him in incredulity.

Florian picked up the telephone and dialled Mireille's number. Her familiar singsong voice replied.

'Hello?'

164

'It's me,' Florian said.

'Oh darling –'

'Listen. I'm with your husband, he's right here. He's been talking to me and I've realised just how much he loves you. I love you too, but not nearly as much as he does. So – I'm taking off and you won't see me again.'

'But – you must be joking,' said Mireille.

'No. Here he is.'

He passed the receiver to the husband, who stared hesitantly at the white plastic, which he at last clamped to his ear.

'Mireille . . .' he murmured.

Florian took back the receiver.

'Faced with love like his, one can't compete,' he said. 'You'll forget me and I'll forget you. So let's forget each other. Goodbye, Mireille.'

He hung up.

'Here,' he said, passing across the revolver. 'Have your toy back. But don't do anything silly, right? We'll call it quits then.'

Florian hugged the man fraternally before he went on his way downstairs.

After a few steps the man suddenly halted, hesitated and came back up.

'Take it,' he said, offering Nazulis the revolver. 'Take it. I don't want it any more.'

Florian had almost run out of Lasavin chocolates. Deciding to replenish his supply, he drove over to his favourite shop on Avenue Victor Hugo. He parked.

The girl was peering into the Hermaphrodite boutique, her nose pressed against the window. She was ogling a low-cut dress with red flounces. Nazulis stopped in his tracks the moment he saw her.

Working from the pavement up, Florian successively appreciated and assessed her slim ankles, the curve of her calves, sturdy thighs, and a waist that was not too narrow but just how he liked it. He could not of course see her breasts, although he imagined they would be rounded and on the small side. Her neck, on which a mass of ringlets and corkscrew curls descended, was entrancing. It seemed designed for lips to kiss. Shortish frizzy hair, chestnut with blonde streaks, crowned all.

'Very attractive from the rear,' Florian reflected. 'Twenty-two or three? What colour might her armpit hair be? And how about her sex-life,' he mused. 'Certainly active, what with an arse like that . . . Not to mention the rest of her . . . Likes to fuck, no doubt about that . . .'

She caught the voyeur's reflection and turned from the shop window with a little smile of complicity. A dimple by the corner of her mouth, and a slight flutter of the eyelashes.

'Even better, front view,' he thought delightedly. Then, looking downwards at her face, he took in her fringe and the light brown hair bleached almost blonde by the sun. Her nose, small and absolutely straight, was a nasal paragon. Her eyes were not exceptional, but they were friendly and warm – greenish, with a twinkle in them. Mouth enticing. Neck: already inspected. Her breasts were fuller than he had expected. He dwelt for a moment on their nipples, clearly outlined beneath the grey cashmere sweater. She wore a tartan skirt with one of those cheeky outsize safety-pins. Shapely knees. Calves and ankles: previously noted. Indeed, the whole verso-recto inspection process had lasted no longer than three seconds. Life, as Florian was well aware, is all too short.

'Listen,' he said. 'I haven't the energy for a lengthy speech. I like you, life's great and we must take advantage of the fact. God does not exist. You are a form of divinity. I feel I want to caress you, make you come, and share my pleasure with you.'

He paused for breath.

'But I don't,' he added, 'love you.'

He drew closer to her, sniffing her fragrance.

'I do love you,' he went on. 'I mean, no . . . It's all too complicated . . .'

He took her arm. She offered no resistance.

'Your place? Mine?'

'I've very little time,' she said.

Florian looked around him. The Avenue Victor Hugo was lined with blocks of luxury flats. He drew her inside one of these. They took the lift to the first floor. A single door with its bell. Florian rang.

No one in. He rang again, then raised her tartan skirt. He pulled down her panties, ran a hand between her legs in casually exploratory yet appreciative fashion, and with an equally fluent gesture took a surreptitious sniff at his fingers. A very healthy scent. One which immediately had Gulliver straining at the leash.

She leaned back against the wall, offering her mouth. He kissed her. Her lipstick had an aroma of raspberries.

Still keeping her skirt hitched with his left hand, Florian undid his belt. His pants and trousers slid down and Gulliver rubbed his head against that curly, rather coarse mane, which tickled and scratched simultaneously. The girl was smaller than Nazulis, so he bent his knees to work his way inside her. She began moaning.

'Not so loud!' he whispered in her ear as he glanced anxiously at the floors above.

'Oooh . . . oooh!' exclaimed the girl.

Gulliver was in full swing. Nazulis meanwhile

168

had slipped a hand under the cashmere and was caressing her breasts. He felt each nipple harden against his palm. He moved up, armpit-wards. Shaved, alas. Still, you couldn't have everything. We won't be choosy about that, he thought.

'Oooh . . . Huuuuh . . . Mmmmm . . .' she was crooning.

Florian's legs were braced wide apart so he could gain maximum penetration. He made no effort to hold back. After all, they had to be quick. The girl too was clearly about to come. Her back jammed against the wall, she had gripped the stranger's shoulders and her head was nodding frantically, gasping nonsensical 'No's' of acquiescence to the pleasure beginning to flood her.

He hoisted the girl's thighs, grasping them firmly with both hands. That way his own posture was straighter and more comfortable – his legs had been seizing up. The girl was not too heavy and all her weight bore down upon the stiffened shaft of Gulliver, now churning dementedly into the oiled maw of that generous snatch-patch.

Her mouth opened, this time with no sound. Her expression turned to an intense, preoccupied rictus. She was now in the throes of climax.

Digging his nails with fiercely luxurious delight into her thighs, Nazulis began thrusting even harder. He shot off, joyous jets of jissom inundating the delta.

He set the girl down. They rearranged their clothes in silence and emerged from the building. She gave Nazulis a swift kiss on the lips.

'Bye!' she said. 'That was nice.'

She dashed away, actually at a run. She seemed to be late. Unlike some obsessive cranks Florian was not a great devotee of the quick fuck. It was all right from time to time, though: no need to be too high-principled on that score.

He would have liked to drop into the Lasavin shop, but it was closed. Too bad: life was pretty sweet anyhow. He finally readjusted his belt. What a rush it had all been.

The Victor Hugo pigeons swooped from the clear sky. They fluttered and flapped their wings ferociously as they tried to peck at the crumbs an old lady had scattered over a bench. One of them soon laid down the law and gave the weaker ones a series of vicious pecks. Nature, thought Florian, is definitely not democratic.

The great wheel of the zodiac was turning. It was the month of May, and soon the trees would become even lovelier, the pigeons fly higher still. The girls would wear progressively less. Flowers would blossom everywhere.

Every day Florian felt happier at being alive. He would wake up to find his friend Gulliver invariably erect and sensitive. The latter too derived such sheer joy from existence that sometimes he even shed a little tear.

The train was on its way to Burgundy. Nazulis winked at Florence.

They were alone in a compartment for eight. Florian had closed the door and drawn the plastic curtains, thus insulating them from the corridor.

Florian's destination was Beaune. The oenologist was scheduled to tour the region arranging orders for the Burgundian growers. This trip would coincide with a big dinner for four hundred people, given by the Brotherhood of Tastevin Chevaliers.

As for Florence, she was going on to Mâcon to visit her sister-in-law who'd just had a baby.

Florian and Florence had managed to co-ordinate their trips. (Travelling together, Florian maintained, was the nearest they got to domesticity.) The lovers had not seen each other for over a week. As soon as the curtains were drawn they fell into each other's arms and embraced passionately. Florian in ecstasy inhaled the scent of the young woman's skin, hair and neck, while their hands eagerly clasped and groped and roved over one another's bodies. He tugged at the

171

sleeves of her silk blouse.

'Take it off,' he said.

'Do you think we can . . . in the train?' she asked.

'Train, car, plane, balloon, troika in the snow, camel's back in the desert, on top of an elephant in the jungle – I'd make love to you no matter where, my love.'

She was wearing a brassière and Florian made her raise her arms. Ah what bliss, the two little thickets had sprouted at last! He breathed their aroma fervently. Like a mother recognising her brats he discerned Florence's own special scent, a freshness of pinewood in sun and various perfectly blended odours he did not attempt to classify. He drank her in, just as she was, high on her fragrance. Gulliver bristled.

'Put your hand on him,' Florian requested. 'He's going bananas.'

She readily complied, placing her hand between the man's legs.

'Don't move,' he said.

They waited until Gulliver calmed down again.

'Take off your bra,' he said.

Right elbow raised, left arm behind her back, she undid the white wisp of material, the fingers of both hands meeting at the mother-of-pearl (or more probably plastic) catch. The bra was removed, and those small breasts, so firm and shapely, displayed.

'Why do you insist on wearing bras?' he asked her.

'My husband's orders,' she said. 'Naked breasts shock him.'

Florian sighed, looking up to the heavens – and yet again appalled by human folly.

'Now your skirt,' he said.

'Do you really think . . . .'

'Yes.'

She unfastened her skirt, stepped out of it, folded it and laid it along the luggage rack.

'Tights too,' he said.

She slid them off. She was now clad only in her cotton panties with their pattern of bees.

'And those,' he said finally.

She hesitated.

'But what if the collector . . .?'

'He'd be only too glad to get a glimpse of a body like yours while he was clipping our tickets. He'd remember the 8.50 from Paris to Mâcon and Lyon, and this Tuesday 15th May, for ever. You're an unforgettable woman.'

She took off the panties and Florian gazed at her nude body. She seemed to him even lovelier and more desirable than that first time.

He undressed hastily and flung his clothes into a corner of the compartment in a heap.

They were face to face, both naked and

burning with desire, but they still did not fall upon one another. Florian was savouring the wait, prolonging the delicious suspense. Gulliver resembled the proverbial ramrod.

Meanwhile the train was shunting slowly on. The telegraph posts flicked past one by one. Florian's hand rested on Florence's shoulder. His fingers descended, toyed with a nipple, dallied down her stomach and reached the silky fleece.

'Ye gods I'm randy,' he said.

'Come on Florian,' she murmured.

She pulled him against herself.

'What position?' he wondered. 'The seats are too narrow . . . Standing up? That'd be too shaky . . . I've got an idea. Let's try a variation – we can call it getting into training – if you just face me, on your knees on the seat, yes, like that . . . Spread your legs a bit wider, that's it.'

Knees parted, her heels tucked under her buttocks, and her back straight, Florence seemed to be engrossed in yoga meditation. She turned up her palms and thus it was that Florian penetrated her.

When fully inside her he stopped moving.

'Can you feel me?' he asked.

'Oh yes!'

'Do you like it?'

'Oh yes!'

They remained as they were for a long while.

Nazulis's nostrils did not cease quivering, sniffing, inhaling the various different aromas released as the young woman's excitement grew. He again made her lift her arms so he could brush his nose against her odorous oxter tufts.

A train running parallel to theirs slowly drew alongside. One by one its coaches passed their own. Then the speed of both trains was identical. They ran side by side in leisurely fashion.

A few feet away on the other side of the glass, a woman was knitting with a sort of tight-lipped fervour, her nose deep in her patterns. Opposite her, her husband was reading the financial page of *Le Monde*. Suddenly the woman looked up, glancing abstractedly at the train next to hers. Her eyes goggled in shock and a hand flew to her mouth.

'She saw us,' Florian said blithely, coupled to Florence as he was, with his nose truffling from one treat to the next.

The owl-eyed knitter tugged her husband's sleeve urgently. The man raised his head with the kind of exasperated grimace one makes in the throes of constipation. His wool-piercer nodded meaningfully, causing him to look to his right. His eyes met Florian's.

'Hello! Hi!' waved the latter.

The dumbfounded needle-clicker and her consort were staring at them in a state of utter incredulity.

'Ecstasy is not merely mystical!' Florian shouted at them.

They could not hear him in any case. Florian started fucking joyfully, thrusting with vigour against the kneeling girl. From time to time he would turn towards the other train which stayed more or less directly opposite.

'Pretty nice, eh?' he signalled to their neighbours.

But then the other train began pulling ahead and they found themselves opposite a new window, at which were clustered half a dozen youthful faces aged from seven to twelve. They were elbowing and jostling, leaping onto the seats and waving their arms in feverish excitement.

'Children aren't shocked by nudity or love,' Nazulis declared, pausing a moment. 'They're only upset when their family circle is disrupted. It's the parents' squabbles which disturb the children. That's our tradition. That's what causes the damage, especially at the start of puberty.'

The train opposite them continued putting on speed. New windows whipped past, along with new faces – whether stunned, shocked, admiring, envious or apoplectic. One granny applauded enthusiastically when she spotted them. A young wife smiled even as she blushed.

176

'Hello!' Florian mouthed.

A sourpuss angrily pulled down a blind. An adolescent hastily slipped a hand into his pocket.

'Hello, hello!' Florian repeated, waving amicably to each as he calmly continued to copulate.

Then came the rear brake van and the mail-waggon. Nazulis mimed a final greeting for all those love-letters lying inside their sacks, within the armoured strongbox on wheels.

Florian alighted at Beaune.

'Don't forget me,' he said after a last kiss.

'Oh no,' she said 'I won't forget you.'

The train drew away. Florian waved goodbye briefly, his heart heavy. Behind the glass Florence, looking like a small child about to cry, waved and signalled back. The train disappeared into the distance. Sometimes, he thought, it was painful to love. Yet you couldn't love without some pain. As he headed down into the tunnel he said to himself: 'All things considered, though, one must love.'

9

THE MAID OF BURGUNDY

A car arrived for him at the station. Paul Michelon, a well-established Burgundy wine producer, and owner together with numerous other growers of several vineyards in the Clos de Vougeot commune, had turned up. Michelon was a white-haired, ruddy-hued sixty-five year old. His nose, true, was somewhat purplish, but he was still a handsome man, whose blue eyes sparkled with sardonic humour. A man full of enthusiasm for his profession and with a corresponding zest for life itself.

He hugged his godson in the Brotherhood: this role he had assumed since Florian's induction as a member of the Tastevin Chevaliers. As the two men greeted each other, Paul said:

'Let's see what shape you're in. Put out your tongue.'

Florian complied.

'You don't drink enough. You're not breathing

decent clean air . . . Ah, you Parisians are all crazy . . . Well, what about the women? Everything all right as far as that side of things goes? Getting enough?'

'No problem there, that's for sure,' Nazulis assured him.

Along the Beaune road leading to Dijon they drove between thriving vines. Between rows of the most famous plants in the wine world men and women were turning over the soil for the third and last tilling of the year.

'May I open my window?' Florian asked.

'Go ahead. Do you want to smell the old place again?'

'Yes,' Florian said.

Sometimes he regretted being born in Paris and not having roots in the soil. His roots, he thought ruefully, were in concrete. Now, nose to the window, like a hunting-dog he scented the various aromas of the region. Aloxe-Corton, north of the Côte de Beaune, followed by the first vines in the Côte de Nuits-Préneaux, Nuits-Saint-Georges, Vosne-Romanée . . .

A Mercedes overtook them. The driver, elbow out of his window, was smoking a cigarette.

'Rothmans Red,' murmured Florian.

'You've still got an excellent nose, I see. Are you sure it's Red brand not the Blue?'

'Sure,' Nazulis said. 'The smoke of the Blue

variety is stronger, more tobacco to it, somehow.'

'What about the most expensive sort?' Paul asked. 'The Venezuelan or Saudi style?'

Florian grinned, pulling a face.

'I like you a lot,' Paul said. 'You're almost a son to me, you know.'

Florian, who kept his deepest emotions discreetly veiled, was embarrassed.

'Do you know that?' Paul went on.

'Yes . . . Look, the vines are really beautiful right now, aren't they . . .'

The wind in his face, he was breathing that pure and noble air from slopes which had once belonged to the Dukes of Burgundy, and before them to many generations of humbler winegrowers. For more than two thousand years without a break father had passed on viticultural lore to son, and whole lives had been dedicated to producing the magnificent wines now exported all over the world.

'Do you see those vines on the right?' said Paul. 'They used to belong to Monsieur Vinca and from them he produced one of the best wines in the entire region. His family had been in the wine business for over five hundred years. Now the son has gone to live in Paris and he's an estate agent.'

'The shit,' Florian muttered. 'Fancy abandoning all this just to flog mass-produced hovels.'

The car arrived at the small commune of Vougeot. Whenever French Army units passed the approaches to these particular vineyards they would traditionally halt, stand to attention and salute.

They drove past several old houses and took a small road lined with trees and vines. Then they reached their destination.

Delightedly Florian re-encountered the special odour of the old house: the ancient furniture still smelled of fresh wax. He climbed upstairs to his usual room, a tiny attic. There he found the same flowered bedspread; those same seventeenth century beams cracked, pitted and blackened by time; and that same wardrobe with the creaky door. Beside the door someone (and he thought he discerned the feminine touch) had placed a small vase full of wild flowers.

Before setting off on his business rounds, Florian swiftly changed his shirt, socks and underwear. Next to his skin he liked fresh clothes at all times. He didn't bother overmuch about the rest – old trousers, a leather or corduroy jacket sufficed.

'Off on your rounds?' asked Paul. 'You can use my car.'

'Yes, thanks. I've a big notebook of orders to fill out. Wine's selling quite cheaply at the moment, despite or because of the economic recession. I have to go to Gevrey-Chambertin and Chambolle.'

'When you get back I'll try you with something you'll enjoy tasting, then we'll have dinner at the Brotherhood.'

'I'm sure it'll be a great evening,' Florian said.

Florian's work was very tricky. He could not afford to make any mistakes and indeed there was simply no room for error. The quantities he would order for his American, German, British or Japanese buyers involved hundreds of hecto-litres, discounts of millions of centimes and so on. It was all basically a matter of buying the finest wines at the best prices.

From the outset of these buying trips, Florian Nazulis allowed himself no lapses, no latitude. He never drank: he tasted. He concentrated only on choosing the wines, forgetting or ignoring women, the flowering hillsides and the multifarious pleasures of life at large. At these times he played the uncompromising wine-expert, tough and absolutely single-minded – a real professional.

Apart from his professionalism, Florian was the possessor of an olfactory sensitivity second to none and an extraordinary memory. In the Côtes de Beaune and Côte de Nuits areas he enjoyed an enviable reputation. At any blindfold testing he was always sure to excel.

He returned at the same time as the sun's rays have lost their strength and strike obliquely, indirectly, spreading the shadows, buildings, telegraph poles, vines and fences lengthwise along the earth of Burgundy.

He rejoined Paul, who was seated at a chess-table in the big ground floor drawing-room. Facing his friend sat a young girl, lost in thought and with her head in her hands. She rose when Florian appeared.

'No, don't get up,' he protested. 'You're in the middle of a . . .'

'Don't you recognize me then, Monsieur Nazulis?' said the girl.

He had not recognized her.

She was small, almost petite, with long brown hair untidily tumbling over her shoulders. She had dreamy, rather nebulous eyes, which gave her an unfocussed or even inexperienced expression with its own youthful charm. She had an unusual, pouting mouth with extraordinary lips. These were almost negroid – upper and lower lips of equal thickness. Her chin was rounded, and her whole face showed she was abruptly moving from child to adult. It seemed too that the transition – as far as the physical side went, at least – was progressing nicely. The young girl's only blemish was a tiny scar on the right side of her forehead.

'No, it can't be,' Florian murmured. 'It's not possible. It's not little Est . . .'

'It is indeed,' Paul said.

'Estelle!' Florian exclaimed. 'Last time – '

She was smiling.

'The last time I – ' Florian went on in astonishment ' – Well, yes, time flies I know, but this is ridiculous!'

'You haven't changed,' she said.

'So much the worse for me,' he said. 'My God how pretty you've become! Well, well . . .'

He took a step back to have a better, admiring look at her.

'Just watch yourself, lad,' Paul joked. 'I know what you're thinking.'

'Look Paul, she's only a child . . .'

'Not at all,' Estelle protested. 'I'm sixteen and a half.'

'She's been helping out here since leaving school. Filling in before getting some more interesting work. This way she earns some pocket money . . . Estelle, can we adjourn the game, if you don't mind? I'd like to show Florian something. Bring us a couple of glasses and that bottle

I put out.'

'Right, Monsieur Michelon.'

'Amazing how attractive she's grown!' Florian commented when she disappeared – and she had moved like a Burgundian ballerina over those red floor tiles.

She returned with large, deep glasses beside which she placed the bottle Paul had opened in his guest's honour.

'I should warn you,' said his host. 'that this is not just any old plonk.'

'I should hope not,' said the oenologist.

At that hour the room was getting darker and Florian had difficulty checking the wine's colour, but when he raised and rotated his glass, sniffed the liquid and finally rolled it around his tongue, when with his eyes still closed he swallowed the first mouthful – he found himself lost for words. Quite speechless, he simply pointed at the bottle in sheer disbelief.

'Mmm?' Paul said. 'Not bad, eh?'

'Fantastic,' Nazulis muttered. 'Where oh where did you find this one?'

'A mystery,' Paul said, forefinger to his lips.

Florian again brought nose to glass, sniffing with tiny quick inhalations, then after another ritual and reverent swill, he at last drank again.

'Fabulous,' he pronounced. 'A Romanée-Conti. A bottle like this must be worth a fortune.

186

You're crazy, Paul.'

'What year?'

'At least twenty-five years old. Probably a '59.'

'Correct.'

'It's only the second time I've ever drunk it. Sharing a Romanée-Conti has become an exceptional event. That year the output was infinitesimal, was it not?'

'Hardly two hectares,' Paul said.

Nazulis was moved almost to tears. Paul had to pat his shoulder gently.

'Come on Florian! Here, drink a bit more. You're right, though: we have here one of the great Burgundies.'

'From one of the greatest years of the century,' Florian added.

Estelle had remained discreetly at the far end of the room.

'You really must taste this,' said Nazulis. 'A wine like this – well, you understand . . .'

He could not find words to continue.

'I don't know much about it,' she said shyly.

'Here, drink some of mine,' Florian said. 'First enjoy the bouquet, then try just a little on your tongue and let the wine move around your mouth . . . And savour it! You won't often have the chance to drink such a magnificent wine. It's priceless – and no longer even for sale, I should think – '

'Subtle yet strong, eh?' said Paul, his eyes twinkling. He was holding his glass at eye-level, as if it were a chalice.

'What smoothness and fullness!' he exclaimed after drinking.

'You might say it was a feminine wine,' Florian commented. 'Plenty of body but not brash or sharp . . . what a magnificent vintage! What do you think of it, Estelle?'

'It's really nice,' she said.

Florian refilled his glass and turned it between his fingers. Again he inhaled, assessed, enjoyed, closing his eyes to drink more.

'More bouquet than Romanée-Saint-Vincent,' he said, reopening his eyes. 'And more finesse than the Richebourgs . . . It's truly the king – or rather queen – of all the Vosne-Romanées. A queen of Burgundy.'

On the horizon the sun was poised behind hills covered with flowering vines: it was bidding the earth goodnight.

Florian, accompanied by Estelle, was strolling between two rows of vines on the crest of a hill.

'Look,' he said. 'It's sinking.'

The red sphere slowly dipped.

For a second or two Florian felt a twinge of

something close to panic, as he so often did when the sun was about to disappear from the sky. Then, as suddenly as the anxiety manifested itself, it passed. He took Estelle's hand and they carried on walking.

There was a large stone beside one of the vines and they sat on it and watched night fall.

'What are you thinking about, right now – at this very moment? Don't even pause, tell me quick!'

'That's a secret,' she said.

'A boyfriend? Fiancé maybe?'

'No, not at all,' she smiled.

He clasped her hand and played with her fingers. He realised she was taking a sidelong glance at him but it was too dark for him to interpret that glance. With his other hand he began stroking her long hair. She remained immobile.

He leaned forward and kissed her cheek lightly. Then he kissed that cheek more firmly and still she made no movement. He tilted her chin, drew her towards him and put his lips to hers. Hers were warm and full, and for as long as he was kissing her she let him, remaining absolutely passive.

His need for her was brutally sudden and urgent. He lifted her into his arms and carried her to a grassy patch nearby. This was the very spot on which, centuries past, Gontran, King of

Burgundy, had waved at the surrounding vineyards and announced to the Abbé de Saint-
Bénigne: 'It's a gift!'

'But – ' the cleric had stammered.

'It's for your monks. Your wine for Mass . . .'

As he lay on top of her Florian continued
kissing her, then he began undoing her blouse.
He slid his hand inside and caressed her breasts,
which were well-developed for a sixteen-year-
old. He then undid her blue jeans.

'No,' she said.

'Don't you . . .'

'I can't . . . I've never . . .'

Florian had managed to slip his fingers against
her tufted mound, but it was tautly enclosed by
her panties. He went on trying to remove these,
tugging first at one side then the other.

'No, no!' she kept protesting.

'Why?' Florian asked, his desire becoming
rapidly uncontrollable.

'I don't . . . haven't . . .'

'But listen . . . No! . . . Wait!'

They were rolling over in the grass, struggling,
their bodies tightly entwined. Florian succeeded
in removing her blouse, and despite the gathering
blue-black darkness he could discern the ample
apples of her breasts. He kissed them fervently,
admiring them and weighing, fondling with both
hands.

She tried to evade him but he pinned her to the grass. Lifting her arms he obeyed his olfactory obsession and plunged his nose to her oxters. He sniffed the downy patches there beneath her arms. A piquant mixture of certain odours led him to believe that she wanted to: wanted to, him, it! She was moist with desire, with wanting to make love.

'I've never . . .' she repeated.

'I'll teach you,' he breathed.

'No . . . I don't . . .'

He finally got her zip undone. She was struggling. As she did so, he kept pulling at one leg and then the other, trying to tug off her jeans. But jeans closely moulded to a girl determined to resist are an impregnable barrier.

He managed to slide his hands between her legs, which were flailing and thrashing about. She was sopping wet, oozing a lukewarm liquid, and Florian wondered if she had her period: no, he decided, he would have recognised the scent of that . . . It was desire, no doubt about it.

His hand bore down upon the light fur, maintaining its exploratory pressure despite her efforts to break away.

'No, no!' she repeated.

While she fought him he tried to sink his fingers into the moist folds. Suddenly she no longer struggled. She seemed to surrender and her legs

191

went limp. She allowed him to take off her jeans, then her panties. She was quite naked now, but he could not see her properly. Night had fallen and the moon was not yet visible. A fresh evening breeze blew through the vines and in the distance faint noises could be heard from the various growers' houses.

Florian undressed in seconds and lay upon the supple, resilient body still (so it felt) with its layers of puppyfat.

'I can't make love,' she said.

'Why not?'

'I want to stay a virgin.'

'Why?'

'I want to stay a virgin.'

Florian could feel her chest heave, hear her rapid respiration. Gulliver, squeezed along her furrow, was exuding a transparent oil which trickled down the young girl's sparse pubic fleece.

'Stay a virgin?' repeated Florian in disbelief.

He moved his fingers over the sodden aperture, stroking her expertly with his fingertips and rotating these in a slow, regular rhythm.

'No, no . . .' she murmured.

Under his hand the moisture was so copious that the tops of her thighs were now soaked.

'I don't want to . . .' she was stammering.

He laid his mouth on her vertical mouth, placing his own lips on her nether lips. Her young girl's scent excited him to an unprecedented lustful fervour. He thought he was about to go crazy.

Putting out his tongue he immersed it fully in her cleft. Then he flicked it to and fro, drinking deep of that aromatic fluid which oozed from her like a subterranean spring. He tried to go deeper still, thrusting his tongue forward – but it found the hymen blocking its way. Determined to persevere, he decided to deflower her lingually if need be . . .

'I don't . . . want to . . .' she begged.

Tongue probing taut, mouth clamped avidly over her mound, he was welded to her in an inexorable buccal embrace. The adolescent body suddenly tensed, jerked upwards and remained in rictus, arched off the ground. What luck, he thought, and what bliss too: she was coming.

She emitted a sigh, a sort of sob, then a little puppy's yelp. He felt welling into his mouth the waves of her ecstasy. A new taste mingled with the previous flavour, this time with the scent of fresh-caught prawns.

She thrust her hands through Florian's hair and her body relaxed. They lay there without moving in the darkness of the night.

'Look at the stars,' she said.

He rolled over to lie on his back, pressed closely against her.

'Do you know the names of the stars?' she

asked.

He took the girl's hand and placed it on a Gulliver rigid and slippery with desire.

'It's vast,' she said.

'The night?'

'No, *that*,' she said.

He initiated a gentle motion to and fro against her hand.

'Stroke it,' he said.

'I didn't know an orgasm could be so strong,' she said. 'You made me feel something . . . something . . .'

'Mmmm?'

'Overwhelming.'

'Like an earthquake, was it?'

'Or a tidal wave,' she said.

He repositioned her small hand round Gulliver, her palm cradling his fiery head.

'Yes, use your hand,' he requested her, 'yes, that's fine, like that, go on . . .'

An owl began hooting plaintively far off towards Chambolle. A plane flew by, very high up in the sky now filled with stars. He had a sudden urge to penetrate her. Rolling over, he lowered himself upon her, Gulliver at vulva.

'No, no! I don't want to . . .'

He bore down harder and its tip brushed the soft thicket.

'No, Monsieur Nazulis.'

'Florian,' he corrected her.

She tried yet again to evade him but he held her firmly by the wrists. The oenologist's body was wedged in place between the girl's legs. Gulliver's glans approached the humid gully.

'No, no,' she was repeating.

The head dug in a centimetre or so while Nazulis continued holding the adolescent in a vice-like grip.

'I'm going inside you,' he announced.

'No!' she shouted.

Gulliver half-inched forward. A fraction further and the lips began admitting the rounded stave.

'I'm in you,' Nazulis said. 'Don't tense up . . . Let yourself go . . .'

He advanced again very slightly and Gulliver's tip encountered the elastic resistance of the hymen. The tightness of the passage and the taut membrane were proving obstacles, despite the ample lubrication of the whole area. Florian dug in deeper.

Gulliver's bald pate had now completely entered. The hymen resisted. The young virgin started moaning.

'It's hurting me . . . it hurts . . .'

'It must do,' Florian murmured, kissing her mouth even as it complained.

The owlet again began to hoot. A sudden breeze made the young girl shiver. Florian held himself

195

poised rigidly above her, about to plummet hawk-like down.

'Now,' he said.

10

JANE AT THE CLOS DE VOUGEOT

With a deep, straight thrust he sank into her, his gradual yet firmly controlled advance ensuring that he slid inside her to the very hilt. She uttered a cry. A bird took wing, flapping upward in a sudden rush. A dog began barking in a nearby village and was echoed by another.

Silence again fell on the hillside of Clos de Vougeot.

Florian stayed stiffly ensconced within the young girl and there he remained, motionless.

'Did it hurt?' he asked her.

'A bit,' she said, running her fingers through her lover's hair. She pulled Florian's head down and kissed him passionately. A real, prolonged and fervent kiss – upon the very soil tilled by those monks whom Gontran's royal gift had delighted.

All these vines had guaranteed them a constant supply of wine for their religious services. And what wines! During the centuries which followed, the kingdom of the Burgundians became the Duchy of Burgundy. The various religious orders still controlled the region's vineyards: Chassagne, Savigny, Aloxe, Santenay, Pommard, Meursault . . .

The couple quivering in love's spasms between the vines were merely links in an endless chain. Nazulis devoutly hoped that the soil of Burgundy would go on favouring wine and love forever.

Still joined to Estelle, he was now moving a little, very gently working Gulliver back and forth in the close-fitting scabbard of flesh.

'I'm not hurting you am I?' he asked her.

'Hardly,' she whispered. 'You're doing me good. That's fine now, like that, go on . . . I like it, I like it . . .!'

He plunged slowly and deliberately, to the hilt again, pulled back and almost out of her, then back deep once more, held by those warm, sleek, clinging walls.

'I don't suppose you're on the pill, are you?' he inquired.

They burst out laughing, bumping heads in mutual surprise at such merriment, Florian all but slipping out of her.

'So when – '

'I had a period three days ago,' Estelle said.

'There's no need to worry, then,' Florian

concluded.

Immediately the muscles, nerves and blood vessels hitherto so firmly controlled by Florian relaxed. A pack of ecstatic greyhounds seemed to leap forward, unleashed at last, in full cry.

'I'm going to come,' he murmured.

'Come,' she said.

She was so tight that Florian, on feeling this continuous constriction, had the delectable impression that he was being squeezed by a pleasure-vice, was melting in a paroxysm worthy of the eleventh century monk Aubin . . . And indeed, on that very hummock of grass where Nazulis and Estelle greedily grappled, a four-teen-year-old girl was once tumbled long ago by the twenty-five-year-old cleric.

Aubin had been a bawdy and wealthy monk. In mediaeval times he and his colleagues made fortunes from these vineyards. Certain among them had been seduced by material riches away from the strict monastic regime and had led dissolute lives. Aubin was one of these. He was partial to any young female between thirteen and twenty. Aubin would offer them a gold piece and roger them among the vines. Then he would be off to check his accounts and revenue.

In the twelfth century Bernard of Clairvaux campaigned against the widespread lechery and avarice of the monks. He took over and reformed the monastery of Citeaux in 1112, assisted by his own troop of monks, and thus the Cistercian Order came into being. It adopted the motto *Cruce et Aratro* (By Cross and Plough) and the monks undertook to cultivate waste or overgrown land. They planted new vines and viticulture became the Order's main occupation. The Clos de Vougeot was thus constituted, plot by plot, thanks to donations from noblemen impressed by the industrious sanctity of the monks.

The vine nearest the coupling of Florian and Estelle thrust from a soil tilled 2610 times since the coming of the Cistercians, at a thrice-yearly calculation.

It was as if a gigantic hand had sprouted from the vine-tendrils to seize Florian's loins and force them into a veritable crescendo of relentless pistoning power.

'Estelle,' he gasped. 'I'm coming . . .'

'Yes, oh yes, come,' she said, her legs and whole body now fully open to him.

For the first time in her life she felt the male orgasmic spasms spreading inside her, diffusing a wet warmth deep within. She clutched Florian still closer to her.

'Don't move,' she begged him.

Florian had collapsed on top of the young woman. For some inexplicable reason he kept hearing Schubert's Ninth Symphony – the second movement resounded inside his head, performed by full orchestra while his truffling nose, buried deep as it was in the girl's downy armpit, was ravished by her unique and individual aroma.

'Don't move,' repeated Estelle, feeling the man's seed trickle deep within herself.

BONUM VINUM LAETIFICAT COR HOMINUM! The Latin words, declaimed in unison by the four hundred guests of the Brotherhood of Tastevin Chevaliers, reverberated through the great banqueting hall of Clos de Vougeot castle.

When the guests sat down, the echo still resounded in the selfsame place which five centuries earlier had been filled with the monks' plainsong.

There was a brief silence as each guest took his or her allotted seat in this room whose pillars were decorated with coats-of-arms and with ancient sacks commemorating harvests of long ago. Then, rapidly, the atmosphere relaxed.

The Burgundy Association, one of the best known in France, had invited numerous other wine clubs, connoisseurs and growers. Mediaeval costumes; red and white togas; black, yellow and green head-dresses; multicoloured tunics and facsimiles of original historical designs were all in evidence – a colourful and impressive display.

The Companions of Beaujolais. The Knights of Saint-Emilion. The Council of Cupbearers. The Toastmasters' Association. The Brotherhood of Bacchus. The Gourmet Group. The Worshipful Fraternity of Vintners. The Médoc and Graves Company . . . All these and many others – even the Americans with their Universal Order of the Knights of the Vine of California – were present. Indeed, it was a comprehensive and yet exclusive gathering of food and drink buffs.

Paul Michelon had arranged with the organizers for ·Florian to be seated next to the most attractive woman in the assembly. Good palates are by no means an all-male preserve, and (as well as prominent media and showbusiness folk) the Tastevin Chevaliers had welcomed a select number of ladies with established reputations as connoisseuses of food and drink.

So Nazulis had been placed next to the very vivacious and delightful Jane Kirbin, the Anglo-French singer and actress: she also happened, by a stroke of luck, to be one of the oenologist's own particular showbiz favourites.

She was a slender, almost emaciated woman, whose long brown hair seemed to sweep away whenever her head turned. She was wonderfully blue-eyed and alluring. She had, too, a childish piping voice which wrought some alchemy on Florian's erogenous zones. Usually he preferred better-upholstered women, plumper and more generously endowed about the arse, but Jane had sexual magnetism of an uncommon order and quality.

Florian kissed her hand with impeccable courtesy – they had not met before – and then a young man, a waiter with a red feather on his hat, appeared with the Meursault.

Florian turned towards his neighbour: she raised her glass and they toasted each other. She had such a girlish, entrancing laugh that he felt like climbing up the curtains – thence yelling a wild Tarzan whoop so his Jane would listen to him.

In short, he needed to turn on the charm.

'Do you know,' he asked in a learned tone, 'the meaning of the word "Meursault"?'

'No,' she said.

'Meursault comes from *saut de souris*, mouse jump. There was so little to choose between the white grape vineyards and the adjacent black ones that a mouse could have jumped the gap. Today it's a different story. As you know, Meursault is almost invariably a white wine, apart from a few Noir Pinot grapes here and there . . .'

She listened to him, smiling, her chin resting on her fist.

What, he thought, could he tell her next? He could talk of Chablis, Chiroubles, Moulin-à-Vent, Saint-Amour. But perhaps she didn't like Beaujolais . . .

The *barbillon grillé* was accompanied by a Chablis Grand Cru 1978, a superb wine, then came lobster served with a Pouilly-Fumé, which Florian found disappointing.

'Slightly disappointing, don't you think, the Pouilly?' he remarked to his neighbour.

'You're very particular,' she said, stuffing a lobster sliver between her pretty lips.

'Don't you think it's rather old hat?'

'I beg your pardon?'

'Don't you find it's a bit past its best?'

'I'm not an expert . . .'

'Just trust your instinct,' he said. 'The pleasure your mouth gets from the wine . . . It's a whole world . . .'

He warmed to his theme. He wanted to take her hand and tell her: 'I love you, let's get married and have kids, I'll be faithful, no other woman will exist for me.'

He asked for more Chablis and for the Pouilly to be taken away.

Soon it was the turn of the *fricassée de poulets à l'essence de racines*, and the red-feathered waiter suggested another wine, but Florian preferred to stay with the Chablis.

'Do you mind our sticking to the Chablis before the red wines?' he asked Jane.

'No problem. You're the boss,' she murmured, in that trill that thrilled, her truly prick-stiffening voice.

Meanwhile the great banqueting hall had filled with an ear-splitting and jovial din. Laughter, animated conversations and occasional shouts could be heard the length and breadth of the enormous room.

A rosy cloud floated in front of Nazulis and Jane's beautiful profile blurred somewhat. His head was spinning slightly. Life, he considered, was more than good.

Suddenly he became aware that the President of the Brotherhood was clapping for silence.

'Rest assured,' the latter began, 'that I won't make a long speech. May I simply welcome all the members of the various estimable organizations which have done us the honour of being with us here tonight. We all have a variety of mutual links, but one main common interest unites us this evening – Wine, that right royal beverage, that nectar of the gods, the draught of immortality

. . . It was Bacchus who . . .'

'He's good for at least an hour of this,' Florian whispered in his neighbour's ear. 'It's the same at every banquet: wine is being celebrated but it's virtually impossible to do the subject justice. As with love. How to describe the pleasure of love-making to someone who's never experienced it? What can one say? "This tickles, that scratches, this feels nice, that swells and goes down again"? How does one convey the incomparable sensation of climax? We fall back upon impoverished words which only approximately describe the miracle. These are things one must live, not talk about . . .'

Her big blue eyes were staring at him.

'Do you think I'm an idiot?' he asked.

She shook her head, smiling very genuinely.

'You're an enchantress,' he said, dropping his voice and glancing either side of them to make sure no one heard. 'You're even beyond the *femme fatale* stage . . .'

She suppressed her laughter behind her hands, those slender hands with their long fingers. It would have been bad form to embarrass the President – speechifying in full flow – who was now discussing Dionysiac art, quoting from *The Song of Songs*, touching upon the Grail Legend, and so on.

'You're so . . . such a woman . . . I mean a

woman of such . . .'

He was fumbling for his words, trying to make an impressive and emphatic declaration to this exquisite woman. She interrupted him by leaning across and giving him a kiss. A light kiss, to be sure, but a kiss full on the lips.

'Ye gods,' Florian murmured.

'. . . this modest but profoundly significant shrub of the genus *ampelidaceae*, in a word – the vine . . .' the President persevered.

'. . . she actually kissed me!'

Once again he wanted to give vent to a cry worthy of Johnny Weissmuller in the jungle, to leap onto the table, proclaiming 'Jane! Jane! I love Jane, and, what's more, she kissed me!' But he calmly extracted the bottle of Chablis from the ice bucket and refilled their glasses.

Once again the rosy cloud wavered before his eyes and the room seemed to tremble slightly. Jane had laid her hand upon his own as if it were the most natural thing in the world. Then the speaker ended his oration and was greeted with thunderous applause.

The next course arrived, borne aloft by a host of waiters all looking like Robin Hood and his merry men. It was *perdreaux à la Sierra Moréna*.

Still floating on his cloud, Florian savoured the aroma of Madeira, bacon and cloves. A Chapelle-Chambertin 1970 was served which, paradoxically, sobered him up. The rhyme was generally axiomatic and well-established that ran:

White after red, easy to bed.

Red after white, headache and tight.

– but Florian all too often reacted differently from the norm.

'What do you think of these partridges?' the oenologist enquired of his neighbour.

'I'm full!' she exclaimed, placing her charming hands just below her small breasts – which were slightly pointed but oh so beautifully shaped!

'I wish she meant full of me, and of our ten children,' he fantasised, looking at her slim waist and flat stomach.

She was staring deep into his eyes now.

'I think I love you,' he said.

'Come off it!' she laughed. 'You've had a drop too much!'

'Not at all, absolutely not,' he said. 'And even if I had, would that make it any less true?'

She was scrutinizing this oddball wild-eyed wine-buff with considerable curiosity.

'I love you and there it is,' he reiterated.

'But . . .'

'Come on, let's go, let me take you off to California and we'll plant vines there and I'll give you wines and children . . .'

She burst out laughing again, her laughter so musical that he had to brace himself against the table in order not to float upwards. The waiter refilled their glasses with Chambertin.

'To our love!' exclaimed Florian, raising his glass.

After the various *entrées*, the Robin Hood characters brought in the main course, braised beef garnished with glazed turnips.

'Oh I just couldn't!' Jane cried in her fluting, childlike voice. 'It's simply *too* much,' she went on. Her delightful English accent was fascinating Florian Nazulis.

'I'll eat yours,' Florian hissed into her ear. 'I'm hungry. It's love.'

The waiter was not in the offing, so Florian refilled their glasses with that magnificent burgundy which was Napoleon's usual tipple and which he took on every campaign in huge casks. But the yokel diluted it with *water*! The thought of it made Florian queasy, even in retrospect.

'What do you think of Napoleon?' he asked his neighbour.

'If you ask an Englishwoman that, what sort of a reply do you expect?' she smiled.

'No, no, I'm not talking politics. I was thinking of how he watered down his Chambertin . . . Don't you find that appalling?' he exclaimed. Then he went on: 'Do you love me?'

'But I scarcely know you!'

'All the more reason, then,' he muttered.

He drained his glass.

'The greatest loves are when the lovers don't yet know each other but that spark is there, the essential atom of each person, if you follow me . . .'

She continued to gaze at him with eyes of azure promise.

'You must think me a complete idiot.'

'No, not at all,' she said, putting an arm around him by way of kindly reassurance.

'Oh I can see only too well that you don't really love me as I love you!'

'I like you a lot,' she said, 'but how do you expect . . .? We've known each other only two hours.'

'I can see you don't love me,' Florian said despairingly. 'For once, life's not treating me well!'

He rose to his feet, staggering slightly.

'Where are you going?' Jane asked.

'I don't know. Doesn't matter where. No-where.'

He crossed the great hall filled with people, noise, aromas and roasts. Leaving through the main door he found himself out in the fresh night air. The distant sound of a cuckoo greeted him.

'Hello, cuckoo,' he mumbled sadly.

He went and sat down on a low stone wall a short distance from the big house. One of the

Clos de Vougeot watchmen spotted him and came over to him. He had a moustache and a cap whose peak dazzlingly reflected the lights of the chateau.

'Aren't you feeling well, Monsieur?' he asked.

The man was quite used to large banquets with their customary influxes into this garden.

'No. Yes. It's all right,' Florian said. 'Heart, you know.'

'Would you like me to fetch a doctor?' the man suggested, suddenly anxious and envisaging cardiac arrest, angina and the whole works.

'Not medical, heart,' Florian said. 'The other thing, love I mean . . .'

'Ah!' the man exclaimed with relief. 'Ah, well, that's fine then. All right.'

He disappeared into the darkness.

Florian lay down along the wall and gazed up at the galaxy. Two hundred thousand million stars, only a million of them identified, were scattered across the vast velvety-blue void above the vines. He looked for the various planets – Mars, that big red dot up there, Jupiter, Mercury, Venus, Saturn, Uranus, Neptune, Pluto.

A shooting star floated across the sky, briefly imprinting its evanescence. He told himself to make a wish: 'I want her to join me here, now.'

He turned round and there she was, very close by, standing tall and slim in her black dress sewn

211

with sequins which themselves sparkled like stars.

'You all right?' she asked.

'Fine,' he said. 'Looking at the stars. The zodiac signs.'

Still lying full-length on the stone wall he saw her as in a low-angle shot, a star against the backdrop of stars. Yes, it would have made a marvellous shot, and a fine film too . . .

He noticed that the star's face was leaning over him. Her hair fell over his cheeks, tickling slightly, before he felt her lips on his. A kiss of such gentleness he had seldom if ever experienced.

'We haven't finished our dinner,' she said in her lilting tones.

While the young woman led him back indoors, slipping her arm in his, Florian felt like addressing a few words to life itself. 'I apologize,' he wanted to say. 'I take back everything I said earlier. You're always good to me.'

11

THE SIXTH FORM IN THE GYM

For quite some time Nazulis had been observing the Lycée girls running round the track at the Sports Centre at the Porte d'Orléans. In pink, blue, yellow, red or green tracksuits they were trotting past him, their elbows tucked in, breathing heavily as they ran.

Tall skinny girls with long legs; little plump things; some of them pretty, others less so. Blondes, brunettes, one or two redheads and a coffee-coloured West Indian girl – the entire sixth form was there.

Some of them had taken off their tracksuit bottoms in the interests of freedom of movement, thus displaying their bare legs which flashed by with big strides. Their shorts – quite as short as the name suggests – showed off their buttocks, allowing the spectator to appraise their various posterior curvatures. Florian was writing in his notebook.

Little doe-*derrières* propelled by slender legs, or flat bums atop rounded columns. Scrawny cruppers upon such frail tubular twigs that the spectator might wonder how they didn't snap under the strain of racing against the stop-watch and whistle brandished by their gym mistress. This PE teacher was a grim-faced, solid pro who resembled a Soviet weight-lifter: she had a lantern jaw and a beam broad as a barn-door.

Each girl who passed him left in her wake an individual aroma. Florian was also noting these odours. For some time he had been monitoring a particularly interesting bouquet. The scent originated from a wiry little blonde now on her eighth circuit of the track. Her long straw-coloured hair was kept in check by one of those white *bandeaux* that give any tennis enthusiast the professional look. The pretty face, somewhat flushed from the exertion, had just turned Florian's head for the eighth time. But it was her rounded, well-muscled, pert buttocks moving like twin full moons that really caught his eye. A first-class arse, borne along by strong legs: all in all, a sturdy sprig.

The wolf licked his lips and straightened his Electricity Board cap.

The girls were now coming up for the tenth lap. Their respective scents drifted past him, irritating or delighting his nostrils. Each aromatic waft attested to efforts made, to pleasure or discomfort, unhappiness, struggle, recent orgasm or continual frustration. It was simply a question of

214

differentiating between them, if not confusing them. His keen nose sniffed like an animal's, patient and intent.

The diminutive blonde was racing round the slightly banked bend, approaching Florian – her knees high, legs working like pistons, and her pretty brow furrowed from the strain. She sped by like an arrow for the tenth and last time. The olfactory membranes of the sniffer quivered, transmitting millions of tiny information signals to that curious computer the brain.

The formidable gym mistress, her eyes glued to her stopwatch, called out the times and placings, then grabbed the whistle which hung round her neck and blew three piercing blasts to round up the girls.

The electrical wolf moistened his chops and discreetly followed the line of girls into the gym itself. The moment he entered the sheepfold he was assailed by a heady mix of piquant odours. Girls were taking off their tracksuit tops. Some made a beeline for the showers, others were just hanging around.

The gym itself was steeped in maidenly odours and resounded to the incessant racket of the young ladies. One of them, apparently keener than her companions, was continuing her exercises. She was poised across the parallel bars in a posture which made the wolf drool.

She was doing the splits, more or less: one of her legs resting on one bar, the other on the bar parallel to it. The position of her legs accentuated the jut of the pubescent pubis, though the latter was of course concealed by the thick elasticated knickers. Florian, that lupine but bogus electricity man, thought he could detect a split in the material. When he approached he found that the material had indeed given way under the strain, revealing (to an expert eye) the reddish frizz of youthful pubic fur.

'Have you come to read the meters?' the Soviet-style PE pedagogue demanded.

The wolf started, startled from his reverie.

'Yes,' he said, touching his cap.

'The meters are down there,' the instructress instructed him.

'You have some very gifted pupils,' Nazulis remarked suavely, his smile nonetheless predatory. 'What grace and athletic prowess! I really admire that.'

There was much else he was admiring, he might have added but did not . . .

'You should see them on the trampoline, that's really something!' the meaty gym mistress said. She blew her whistle again. 'Right, that's it for today, girls! I'm off now.'

'Goodbye, Mademoiselle!' shouted a juvenile arselicker who already looked as if her juices had run dry.

'The meters are down there on the right,' the electrician was once again informed.

Then whistle at the ready, watch in hand, and face set, she headed back to the Stadium, where yet another class awaited her.

Absorbed in their chatter of fashions and rock-stars, the girls paid no attention to the blue-uniformed employee observing them. This man in a peaked cap was self-effacing and oh so discreet: why, he even had the run of the hen-coop!

The girls were undressing. A tornado of odours was unleashed. Numerous sebaceous glands exuded their scents and drying perspiration impregnated the air. Florian's head began to reel.

Just then he caught sight of an exquisite creature.

Not the little blonde of the track but a willowy brunette with perfectly oval features, big dark eyes and long almost black hair which she was shaking loose with childlike grace. She took off her games things and revealed her superb nudity. Her skin was smooth and her small breasts with their brownish aureoles tilted upwards. Her tufted triangle was small and black.

The wolf from the electricity board sprang from the shadow and leaped into the changing cabin she had just entered.

217

'Oh!' she exclaimed – at once charmed by this surprise intrusion.

She raised her arms languorously in a provocative twirl worthy of a ballerina, ready to surrender her all to this virile visitor, this randy handy-man . . . Her eyes sparkled at him from the cabin's murky recesses.

Suddenly Nazulis' nose twitched: he was getting a warning signal. The nasal alarm almost syringed his sinuses. Florian grimaced and Gulliver, like an aged Buddha, retracted. From the schoolgirl there emanated an unbearable odour, as of rotting rabbit marinaded in week-old sweat.

Florian turned tail, dashing back to his vantage point, gasping. He forced himself to exhale deeply and expunge from his nostrils the rest of that tainted air. How could one look so ravishing and smell so awful? Perhaps her thinking was reactionary, he reflected in a desperate attempt at comprehension: too much morality and not enough ecstasy . . . Even her nymphomania was somewhat suspect . . . He had to admit, with considerable annoyance, that he was utterly at a loss . . .

The girls themselves were absorbed in their endless gossip and were quite oblivious to his presence: only rock groups could monopolize their conversation.

The attractive blonde of the stadium – who had smelt so delightful – at last appeared, wearing a yellow track suit. She slipped its top over her head, then a 'US Army' tee-shirt followed it, then a small bra. What a pity – she shaved under her arms! For a second she sniffed at one armpit and frowned her displeasure. Florian thought: one doesn't necessarily smell bad when sweaty. You certainly don't, anyhow . . .

The girl took off her tracksuit trousers to reveal tight shorts. Once again Florian found himself admiring her rounded little buttocks. He realised how much he wanted her.

She unzipped her shorts and took off those too. The mound, moulded so tautly under sky-blue panties that were almost a G-string, protruded. The panties were removed, revealing a magnificent bottom.

At this point she noticed Nazulis, sitting in his shadowy corner, devouring her with his eyes. She covered herself with a towel in a spontaneous reflex of modesty.

'I've come to read the meters,' Florian said. 'Don't mind me.'

'Right,' was all she said, and she draped the towel round her neck.

She headed for a shower cubicle. Florian glanced to right and left, then charged after her. He got there just as she was shutting the door, and he quickly slipped the bolt, locking them in.

'Hey!' she cried, 'are you crazy?'

'Don't worry, I'm a good wolf. I don't eat or bite, I lick and suck.'

He sniffed her hair and shoulders and got her to raise her arms.

'You're making a mistake, shaving under there,' he told her. 'It's really out, depilation. Same goes for plucking your eyebrows. You really shouldn't. Promise?'

'Listen, Monsieur,' she began.

'Well?' Nazulis said.

She stared at him through wide blue eyes which shone from the humid murk. She was not shocked, but she did seem surprised.

The sniffer resumed his researches. His nose hovered over the (unfortunately) depilated zones – which still smelt good, however – and descended along the curve of the hips.

'Mmm!' Florian exclaimed happily. 'Superb!'

He knelt down and inhaled the tufty blonde shrine, nose tickling at the silken wisps. He turned the girl around as if he were a doctor examining her. His face was now level with her backside.

'Mmmm! Mmmm!' he repeated approvingly, his nose against the fine convex curves.

He slid further down, nasally inspecting the cleft, then the legs, to end at last with her ankles.

He stood up again.

'You're in the best of health,' he pronounced.

Gulliver had naturally risen to the occasion, bucking and twitching in his pouch.

'Are you on the pill?' Florian asked.

'Of course,' she replied.

'How old are you?'

'Sixteen.'

'No longer young, eh? You'll have to slow down a bit, old girl.'

She began laughing.

'So how old are you, then?'

'A few years older than yourself,' he murmured, 'but let's not go into that.'

'Are you really from the Electricity Board?'

'What do you think?'

'Since you ask, no.'

The adjoining cubicle seemed to be shaking apart with girlish laughter. The door banged. Outside, from the cloakroom, the sounds of voices shrieking, jabbering, giggling and swapping gossip.

In their cubicle, Florian and the girl were kissing. It was quite a kiss, deep, passionate and committed. Gulliver meanwhile strained – through the official blue serge trousers – to rub against the student's hirsute hillock.

'Do you want to make love?' the latter enquired.

'What a question! Isn't it obvious?'

'Your place?' she suggested.

'Here,' he said.

'Oh yes!' she said, her mouth moving back into a firmly exploratory osculation.

Her tongue slithered with Florian's in astonishing ardour. She seemed game enough for anything, if her tongue was to be trusted. Gulliver continued knob-frotting against the adolescent's gorgeous grinder: the girl herself undulated her hips athletically the while.

Florian doffed his peaked cap and hung it on the door-hook. While he was unbuttoning his uniform she perched the pate-warmer on her head and began pulling faces, trying to imitate a Nazi.

'Where did you find it?' she asked.

'The Flea Market. Hundred francs and the uniform thrown in.'

She hung it up again and with no preliminaries seized hold of Gulliver.

'Not bad,' she said.

Florian was thinking how young people had improved since his day. True, examples of outworn morality still persisted here and there, and leech-like religionists continued to corrupt our

222

dear children, but on the whole kids had few complexes!

The schoolgirl inspected Gulliver from as many angles as space and physiology permitted, palping, weighing, lifting, lowering and tugging.

'Not bad,' she repeated.

Florian was momentarily miffed at not belonging to the 'Super' category but no matter, he felt happy as he was – a normal healthy male with a splendid mate.

'Wait!' the girl said.

She knelt and fellated the forward fellow. Yes, thought the delighted Florian, the younger generation was all right by him!

'That nice?' she enquired, looking up at Florian.

'Super!' he attested. 'That's really getting to me. Much more and I'll burst.'

'Do you want to come in my mouth or right inside me?' she asked him.

'Er . . . hmmm . . .'

Even Florian was all but taken aback by such forthrightness.

'Anyway, you haven't got herpes, have you?' she went on.

'No, certainly not,' he protested.

'Shall I wank you a bit, like this?'

She began masturbating him efficiently and with formidable vigour.

'You're really liberated and that's a fact,' Nazulis said.

'Liberated from what?' she asked, never ceasing to shunt Gulliver – gripped firmly in her hot hand – to and fro.

'Listen,' said the almost breathless oenologist, 'wouldn't you like me to do the same for you, perhaps?'

'Oh yeah, of course!' she exclaimed, leaving go of Gulliver. 'Are you OK on oral?'

'I get by,' he said.

'If you like,' she suggested, 'I'll suck you a bit more, unless you'd rather I stuck my finger up you. Do you go for sodomy?'

'To tell the truth – not really,' Florian replied.

'How about dope?' she asked. 'What turns you on?'

'Wine,' he said.

There was a moment's silence. She looked at him aghast, in sheer disbelief. Then she burst out laughing so helplessly that the thin cubicle partition shook.

'Is that you Natasha? Who's in there with you?' a voice enquired from the next door cubicle.

'With the man from the Electricity Board,' she answered. 'How about you?'

'Valerie's here.'

'Are you doing it?' Natasha asked.

'Starting to. Are you?'

'Yeah,' said the schoolgirl.

'Is he any good?' asked her neighbour.

'Not bad,' Natasha said.

The phrase hit Nazulis like a cold shower. He'd forgotten how hard they were, kids this age.

'Want company?' the voice suggested.

'Is that your scene, threesomes – I mean foursomes?' Natasha asked him.

'Well, I –' Florian managed.

'Open the door quietly, easy now . . .' the neighbour instructed them. 'I'll take a quick peep to make sure the coast's clear!'

Two small naked bodies dashed into the cubicle.

'Great!' Natasha said. 'We'll play sardines, have a real orgy!'

'Hello,' said the taller girl, putting out a hand and shaking Gulliver.

They all began squealing with laughter.

'Hey – what are you up to?' asked a girl in the adjacent cubicle.

'Full up, standing room only!' Natasha yelled. 'Right,' she went on, 'Let me introduce my pal . . . er . . .'

'Florian,' said Florian.

'This is Sophie and she's Valerie.'

'He's not at all bad,' Valerie said.

'I prefer you,' Sophie remarked, giving her a prolonged French kiss.

Encouraged by her example, Natasha followed suit with Florian. The latter was beginning to attain a state bordering upon satyriasis. Their four bodies touched, rubbed, stroked each other. Blonde Natasha, dark Sophie, and Valerie – the only one, Florian noted with pleasure, not to shave her armpits. In any case, he felt considerably attracted to Valerie.

Three women at a stroke: Gulliver scarcely knew which way to turn! Impaling them successively was the logical and pleasurable expectation.

Natasha drew breath, momentarily ceasing her deep tonguing. Her two friends however were still locked in their embrace, grinding their bellies together.

'Do you want me to suck you off?' she asked Florian.

Before he could reply she had dived down and engulfed the Gulliverian glans. A wave of pleasure swept over Florian. The kid knew how to do it, all right. Grasping Gulliver by the root with her left hand, she bobbed slowly back and forth, inexorably and unerringly sliding her tongue along the full shaft, deploying its tip to best effect, and using her lips to grip and squeeze.

'Oh . . . ah . . . oh!' he groaned.

Valerie pulled away from her friend and turned her head towards Nazulis.

'You're not bad,' she said. 'I think you're nice.'

While Natasha, kneeling, on the duckboards, continued her suction, Valerie took Florian's face in both hands and kissed him passionately.

Caught between their two mouths Florian was no longer very sure where he was. Down below he experienced a keen surge of pleasure, while up above the sensual kiss went on and on.

'Tickle my clit a bit, will you Sophie,' said Natasha.

Her mouth busy with Florian and her hand with Natasha, Sophie in turn received a caress. This Valerie, while kissing Florian, managed to give her with one big toe extended. The sighs and moans of the quartet merged into a theme with sometimes languorous, sometimes rapid variations, punctuated by soft cries and gasps.

'I'm taking over,' Sophie suddenly declared. 'I'm going to drain you dry.'

At Gulliver's tip Florian felt the new mouth, quicker and more urgent, breathing feverishly.

'Oh . . . Oh . . .' he gasped.

His kiss with Valerie deepened, continued. Before the culminating spasm, which he sensed imminent, he tried his utmost to hold back, savouring the intensity of pleasure diffused and multiplied. He also had a fierce desire to sniff the schoolgirl's armpits. He tore his mouth from hers and got her to raise her arms. His nose dug into

227

the sparse little tuft of fine hair. The musky aroma heightened his excitement.

'Oh no, oh no . . .' he again gasped. 'I'm coming . . .'

Unwilling to be left out, Natasha knelt behind Florian and with quick flicks of her tongue persuaded him to part his cheeks, until she reached the anal rosette.

It was all too much, this *coup de grâce* to the arse.

Sophie's mouth received the blurted spurts, Natasha's tongue felt his shuddering contractions and Valerie delved on, as if reviving a dying Florian by means of the kiss of life.

A few minutes later Nazulis, resplendent once more in his Electricity Board togs, gave Natasha a folded scrap of paper on which he had scrawled his telephone number.

He waved a brief goodbye to the three girls. There was no doubt, he reflected as he walked out of the gym door, that the younger generation was well and truly liberated.

12

THE WAY LIFE GOES

Rosy-fingered dawn had been caressing Florian's shutters for some time before he woke up. Amazing, he thought, Gulliver was still asleep. That was unusual, since Gulliver always stirred before Florian awoke.

Florian's eyes took in the familiar landmarks of the room, while he listened to the sounds of morning and sniffed the air.

'That's odd – I can't smell anything . . .'

He sat on the bed, turning to point his nose in different directions, like an Irish setter.

'Absolutely extraordinary . . . I can't smell a thing!'

He got up and went over to the window, opening both window and shutters. There was a grey mist outside. He inhaled, standing very still, and taking quick little breaths. He waited, then repeated the process.

'Still nothing? Well, well . . .!' he murmured.

He paced round the room for a while uneasily, quite disconcerted, muttering to himself that it just wasn't possible.

He then located a bottle of 1967 Château-Margaux, opened it and thrust his nose to its neck. Nothing. He rushed to find his bottle of Hautes-Côtes de Nuits, which he was keeping for a special occasion. It was just too bad about that: he wanted to make quite sure now – and if he could no longer smell burgundy, well . . .

With trembling hands he turned the corkscrew and drew the cork. Which broke. He tried to fish out the remaining section of cork but it sank into the wine itself. He cursed through gritted teeth, furiously employing the obscenest oaths in his repertoire. Then he poured the precious liquid into a special wine-glass and tried sniffing it. Again, no result.

Panic flooded through him. He dashed into the kitchen and pulled sprigs of thyme and bay leaves from a drawer. He succeeded in breaking a glass tube containing a vanilla pod, spilt some cinnamon, and then laid out small heaps of pepper and assorted spices . . . He had to admit, in the light of the evidence, that his sense of smell had completely vanished.

He slumped into a chair and stared at the floor as if he were the inmate of an asylum, his mind utterly void and his jaw slack.

The sound of the telephone ringing made him jump. It was Sandra.

'How's life with you, poppet? What are you up to? I'd love to see you! Photo-call till 1 a.m. though. Have to rush because they lock us away till then . . . Yes, it's for a cover . . . In profile, facing the sea . . . Starkers . . . Fix me some coffee, will you, and don't get dressed or anything, I'm on my way over!'

Florian moved like a robot. He poured out some Colombian coffee from the tin, along with Evian water, and plugged in the percolator. He heard the noise the machine was making, but he could still smell nothing whatever!

The doorbell rang and he opened the door to let Sandra in. She looked even more stunning than usual, and her sparkling little teeth were in bright contrast to her deeply tanned face. She flung herself into his arms.

'Ah pet, poppet! Kiss me, then.'

It took only a minute before she was nude and nestling in Florian's arms. Florian was staring at the ceiling.

Sandra's head moved downwards and her lips brushed against the drowsing Gulliver. Her little tongue began working upon the torpid creature.

Still nothing.

'Hum,' Florian said, continuing to stare fixedly at the ceiling.

'What's the matter?' Sandra asked him.

'Hum,' he said again.

'Don't you want me any more?'

She stretched out against him, pressing her stomach close into his. Her lips were warm. She was beautiful, infinitely desirable. Yet Gulliver was shrunken and Florian could no longer smell anything and life was in abeyance.

'Don't you want me any more?' Sandra repeated.

'Hmmm,' Florian muttered, eyes still staring at the ceiling.

Then she began to employ every trick in the erotic book. Not even a Sistine Chapel castrato could have resisted such prolonged sexual onslaughts. Her expertise was that of a professional.

Nothing.

'Wonderful!' she exclaimed with sudden rage. 'If you really don't desire me any more, there's no point in my being here!'

She got up and dressed. The door slammed. Florian continued to stare at the ceiling.

After some time he got up with difficulty, as if exhausted. He dressed and went out into the street. Passers by, cars, shops were all wrapped in a sort of mist and he had the impression of blundering around in fog himself.

He reached the Seine *quais* and gazed for a long time at the water flowing past. Feeling listless, empty and drained of all desire he looked blankly at the dazzling flow of grey waters.

Several hours went by and during the afternoon the sky changed. The wind got up, chasing away the clouds. Beside Florian scraps of newspaper and some dust were whisked aloft by a sudden gust. The sun came out. And suddenly a teasing whiff of Miss Dior reached Florian's nostrils.

He stood up and followed the trail of perfume. It emanated from a gorgeous redhead. She was sauntering along as if in no hurry at all. He drew alongside her.

'You smell nice,' he said.

She looked at him coldly. He was sincere enough. She began to smile as he came over closer to her.

'Do you mind?'

His nose pointed in turn at her hair, neck, shoulders as he inhaled the splendid aroma. He breathed in noisily.

'Have you got a cold?' she inquired.

'It's nothing. The remains of one. I was quite badly affected, but it's over now. Come and have a drink with me.'

After flattering and chatting up this delightful

creature, Florian returned home. He opened his letterbox in the hallway and collected his mail.

He placed his letters on the table and put *The Trout* Quintet, with Rudolf Serkin, piano, onto the stereo. He undressed and took a shower, alternating with enjoyment the hot and cold jets. Schubert's genius all but animated the trout, which seemed to flash and leap through the silvery torrent which toyed with both light and life.

He rubbed down his steaming skin with a towel sweetly scented with lavender: tiny sachets of the fragrance, inserted between stacks of linen, had been a tradition with his grandmother.

When the record ended, he pressed a button marked *Incoming Calls* on his answering-machine.

'Well you dirty rat,' remarked a somewhat adenoidal female voice, 'you never called me back! Louse, swine and cad! You can have a kiss anyway. Ring me.'

Who the hell was that, he wondered.

The tape ran on. There was a tone bleep.

'Darling, it's me, Ariane. The River-Berthoux crowd are having a do on Saturday. It should be a really wild party, so I'm relying on you. It's fancy dress – monsters. You absolutely must come . . . Bye-ee!'

There was another tone signal.

'Sadi's are happy to bring you details of their exclusive Oriental carpets offer at bargain prices with . . .'

He pressed *Fast Forward*, until he heard a distinctive female voice. He stopped short, his heart almost skipping a beat: it was her!

'Good morning. Would you care to come to dinner the day after tomorrow?' said the silvery voice with its English accent. 'I'll cook up something, if you're not put off by the thought of English dishes.'

Jane – inviting him over!

Florian performed a sort of neo-Balkan dance, clapping his hands, clicking his fingers and doing knee-bends. Her place: that sublime woman was inviting him to her house!

It was all finally too much. He had to go and open the window and let in some air.

He filled his lungs with fresh spring air and then caught his breath. Framed in the opposite window was a familiar silhouette. And as the curtains were pulled apart Clémence appeared, wearing only a flowered pair of boxer-shorts. Her breasts seemed to wink at him, and he could see against the glass her lips move. Asking him a question. Florian signalled that he couldn't hear her and she opened her window.

'Now?' she asked.

'In an hour's time, my love,' he shouted.

He returned to his answering-machine.

' . . . and I don't understand why, you disappear with no explanation and all of a sudden . . . I miss you, I want to see you . . .' said the taped voice of Mireille.

That, thought Nazulis, was worthy of a Corneille play. My word or my pleasure. Husband or Gulliver. Mireille or no Mireille . . . Well, he couldn't break his promise and yet he really wanted to see her . . . But . . .

'Beep beep, wee! Here's a nice message for you in my nicest voice, right? Well, you dear little answering-machine, when your master returns you can play him this, OK? Sandra to Florian. No hard feelings. Loves him still. Suggests a nude photo-spread in *Penthouse* for the pair of them. Prompt reply appreciated!'

Florian half-turned to inspect himself in the dressing mirror. Had he, he wondered, an attractive bum?

He turned the other cheek, then spotted a letter which had been slipped under the door and which he had not noticed on his return. He opened the envelope. There was a drawing of a big red heart, executed in marker-pen and rather resembling a pair of outsize buttocks. Underneath it was a handwritten line from Florence: *I'm thinking of you, darling.*

Dear, dear Florence of the delectable arse, he

mused . . . Then he remembered the mail.

Feet resting on the table next to the type-written pages of his *Fundamental Thesis*, he slit open the top letter. It contained a sizeable lock of brownish hair. Florian sniffed a few times.

'Little Estelle! My dear, precious little girl!'

The letter was warm and tender and suddenly Florian was back among flowering vines as night fell on the Clos de Vougeot. Again he inhaled, nose pressed against the tuft of hair. Gulliver quivered, recalling that pretty young body as it opened up to orgasm. He reared his head, curious as ever, available and blithe.

'Hey, calm down!' Florian said. 'Plenty of opportunity for that. There's a whole lifetime ahead.'

He opened another window and inhaled deeply. His nostrils twitched, sensing with pleasant surprise a new tang in the air.

'Spring is almost here,' he murmured. 'It smells like spring. Life's not at all bad, at that . . .'

He opened another letter, which the Post Office had forwarded from his previous address.

Grey paper, badly duplicated. The Saint-Honoro Parish Newsletter, rapidly converted to a crumpled ball, described a wide arc across the room before landing slap in the wastepaper basket.

The telephone rang.

A bout of uncontrollable feminine giggles on the other end of the line.

'Hello?' Florian said. 'Ah Natasha, it's you . . . What? Yes, I can hear you . . . Hello Sophie, hello Valerie . . . Yes . . . Tomorrow afternoon, right, of course . . . Yes, that's certainly an attractive proposition . . . What? I can't hear you!'

He pressed the receiver into his ear.

'Girlfriends of yours . . . Well, yes . . . No, on the contrary, why don't you all come along, all six of you . . . What? Yes, right, we'll have a ball, you can rely on me, that I promise you!'

He hung up.

'Bet your life they can rely on us,' he said. 'Isn't that so, my good old trusty Gulliver?'

NEXUS ADULT READS

NEXUS ADULT READS

0352322454	**Forbidden Frolics**	**£2.99**
0352322004	**The French Collection**	**£2.99**
0352317817	**Exploits of a Young Don Juan**	**£2.99**
0352318554	**Flossie**	**£2.99***
0352313390	**'Frank' and I**	**£2.99***
0352316667	**Lascivious Scenes**	**£2.99***
035231530X	**Laura Middleton**	**£2.99***
0352315830	**The Lustful Turk**	**£2.99***
0352310170	**A Man With A Maid**	**£2.99***
0352310928	**A Man With A Maid Vol II**	**£2.99***

Nexus books are obtainable from many booksellers and newsagents. If you have any difficulty tick the titles you want and fill in the form below.

Name _____

Address _____

_____

Send to: Nexus Cash Sales, P.O. Box 11, Falmouth, Cornwall TR10 9EN.

Please send a cheque or postal order to the value of the cover price plus:
UK: 55p for the first book, 22p for the second book and 14p for each additional book ordered to the maximum charge of £1.75.

BFPO and EIRE: 55p for the first book, 22p for the second book, 14p per copy for the next 7 books, thereafter 8p per book.

OVERSEAS: £1.00 for the first book and 25p per copy for each additional book.

While every effort is made to keep prices low, it is sometimes necessary to increase prices at short notice. Nexus reserve the right to show new retail prices on covers which may differ from those advertised in the text or elsewhere.

* NOT FOR SALE IN CANADA